BONES IN THE BELFRY

A Vivianna Luxe Mystery

Carrin Mahmood

ISBN-13: 9798508096465

Cover design by: Carrin Mahmood
Library of Congress Control Number: 2018675309
Printed in the United States of America

This book is dedicated to my husband who loves me even while I'm writing. That can't be easy, I love you!

To my book club. They are a constant source of encouragement, they are creative, supportive, and loving. They're also the first ones to buy my books. But most importantly they're a ton of fun.

To Dianne, Tara, and Tami editing machines one and all.

And to all of you who have mystifying expertise of something unexpected.

CONTENTS

BONES IN THE BELFRY

By

Carrin Mahmood

PROLOGUE

Some call it a tower

And some call it a steeple

Whatever it is

It sits over the people

Tinker's just "Tink"

Without one of these

Snap a picture of you

with this in it please

"Vivi, hurry," Ty begged. "We have to figure this out."

Ty was winded and looked excited. I was thrilled he was enjoying art camp. Like music camp a few weeks ago, he started out thinking it was going to be lame, but this was only Tuesday and so far he seemed to be enjoying it. Presently, their task was to figure out the clues of different items around the church and take the most interesting picture they could once they found them.

"Okay, okay, so what do you think this is?" I asked. Each camper could have one person go with them as an assistant, and Ty had come to the house and gotten me.

I was the house mother, which was really more of an administrative job, at Grace in the Valley Shelter. The acronym was GIV Shelter, which I loved. Ty was a fourteen-year-old guest at the shelter along with his mom Shawna and sister Shayna. Current guests also included Ashlee, an eighteen-year-old mom, and her six-month-old baby Tootsie, and our newest family, Keith, and Kelli along with their six kids, all of whom also had names starting with K.

Ty had been glued to my side for the last few weeks. I recently had a brief stay in the hospital after a murderer pushed me down some stairs. Moments before I had a hunch that he was the one responsible for the dead guys that kept piling up in the shelter. The shove down the stairs confirmed it. Ty thought having dead guys in the shelter "was tight" but had been pretty upset when I got hurt. Like most of the males in my life, he was both impressed and slightly horrified by my means of escape. I had mule-kicked my attacker and inadvertently punctured a testicle with a four-inch, razor-thin, Jimmy Choo stiletto.

In my real life, which I hoped to get back to sooner rather than later, I didn't run a shelter, didn't track down murderers, and certainly didn't do photographic scavenger hunts with homeless fourteen-year-olds. I mostly shopped, attended charity functions with my friends and business functions with my dad. Unfortunately, my dad had left town in the middle of the night like the Baltimore Colts and taken what was left of our money with him. In all fairness, he was being falsely accused of embezzlement, fraud, and a whole laundry list of other things.

I packed what I could of my former life into two moving trucks and was hiding out on the opposite side of town. Pastor Carson Hitchmayer, the lead pastor of Grace in the Valley Lutheran Church, had overheard me telling my best friend, Ezzie Gold, that I was sleeping in a storage unit and offered me the job at the shelter. Ezzie has been my best friend since kindergarten after an unfortunate incident involving Janet Jargotto's head and a carton of milk. She was the only one of my former friends who knew where I was, and frankly the only one who really mattered. Our plan was to find out who was framing Daddy so I could go back to being filthy rich like a normal person, but we'd been side-tracked when I found a corpse in the parlor.

"I think it's the bell tower because Tinker makes me think of Tinkerbell and it's over the people if they sit in church," Ty said.

I thought it seemed like the obvious answer also, and we headed over to the front of the church. Several kids were taking posed pictures or selfies with the bell tower in the background.

"Vivi, it's one point for having the correct clue in the picture, but two points for having an artistic picture," he explained as he had for the last four pictures.

"Okay bud, how do you want to shoot this one?" I asked.

"Let's go up there, and you can get the bell in the foreground and me in the background. It will be different than everyone else's."

We headed inside to check with Mavis to see if that would even be possible. Mavis was the Lead Pastor's support person, and as far as I could see pretty much ran the whole church. She had gotten a job at Grace right out of high school and had been there for twenty years. She had enthusiastically joined Ezzie and me when we were on the hunt for whoever was killing rich guys. Pastor Hitchmayer had been less enthusiastic. In fact, he had been quite loudly unenthusiastic about us sticking our noses into a murder investigation.

"Hey Mavis," Ty said, as we walked into the main office.

"Well hello there Ty. So how are ya doing then?" she asked. Mavis had an almost cliché Minnesota accent. She grew up "On the Range" and sounded like she had been the voice coach for the movie "Up North."

"I'm fine," Ty said politely then turned and looked at me, clearly thinking I would have better luck with this request than he would.

"Mavis, we need a picture of Ty with the church bells. Is it possible to go up to the belfry?"

"Oh sure, that will be a wonderful picture. You can see the St. Croix River from up there, Ty," she said as she handed me her master key. "Just bring me the key when you're finished. You might have to lean into the door a bit, it's been sticking."

Ty and I found the staircase, and he flew up the stairs like they were horizontal. I thought I was in good shape but realized I might have to consider adding some cardio into my workout routine. I tried to ignore my inner voice saying "you should add some 'workout' into your workout routine," and huffed and puffed my way up the last few steps.

Mavis was right, the view was spectacular. You could see all of the GIV property, which included the church, the rec-center, the quaint little barn, now used as a restaurant, the community center, the shelter, and the small but thriving vineyard. On the very edge was a huge labyrinth with a paved path and a small lake with a gazebo and benches. I stood in for Ty as he set up the shot. Ty went to the west side of the tower, and I walked to the opposite side. The bell was between us, as it was going to be the main feature in the shot.

He started giving posing directions like we were doing a cover shoot. "Vivi, stand on your tiptoes so you're more my height."

I wasn't sure that was going to be helpful. At a little over six feet, he was almost seven inches taller than I was, but I stretched as far as my toes would let me. Behind me, the entire St. Croix River Valley stretched for miles, and it was going to be a spectacular shot.

"Vivi, move a little to your right," he said.

"Wuahhhhh," I yelled as I tiptoed over to my right and promptly tripped over a grey nylon Nike bag which I hadn't noticed before.

"Are you okay?" Ty asked, running around the bells.

"Yeah, I'm fine," I said. "I scraped my elbow into the wall, and my tailbone might be kind of sore. . ." I stopped mid-sentence when I saw his panicked face.

"You didn't hit your head, did you?" he asked.

I knew he was thinking about the concussion I had recently had and quickly assured him it was just an elbow and a butt, nothing to worry about. Like any two normal human beings, we turned our attention to the duffle bag and immediately unzipped it to see why it was up in the belfry.

"Shitballs!" Ty gasped.

"Yeah," I agreed, slightly worried about getting struck by lightning due to cursing in the church's bell tower.

"What the hell?" he continued.

"Yeah," I repeated, rather stupidly.

"Mother F. . ."

"Okay Ty," I said, cutting him off. "We should probably go get Pastor Hitch. I'll stay here while you. . ."

"No way Vivi," he said, this time cutting me off. "I'm not leaving you up here with a bag of bones."

We just sat and looked at each other. Both of us had literally been knocked back on our heels.

"Good point, I don't want to stay here alone," I admitted. "We'll just call him." I was not looking forward to this call. I was the one who had found the last dead guy on the church grounds, and now there were clearly human remains in the bag. This couldn't possibly be good for business, or attendance, or whatever they called people coming to church. Hitch was going to be furious. But now that Ty and I had our fingerprints, and my stupid elbow blood and probably tons of who-knows-what kind of DNA all over the bag, we couldn't just walk away. I sent a text to Hitch that said, "HELP! Ty and I just found bones in the belfry!"

CHAPTER 1

Tuesday

Ty and I sat a few feet away from the bag with our knees pulled up to our chins and our backs to the wall. Hitch stood over the bag shaking his head.

"Unbelievable," he said, sounding about ready to blow.

"He sure shakes his head a lot when he's around you, Vivi," Ty stated.

He sure does, I thought. To be fair this was the second time in under a month I had been the one to find a dead body on the church property. I was sure he was reconsidering his brilliant idea of having me be the "House Mother" for the shelter right about now.

"Is that your blood on the bag?" he asked, looking at Ty.

Ty looked terrified so I jumped in, "No, it's mine."

"Of course it is," he said, closing his eyes while shaking his head again. "Are you always this much trouble?"

"Hey, that's not fair. I'm the one who is traumatized here. I should be asking the questions. Do you always have dead bodies popping up all over your church campus? Do you make a habit out of scaring fragile children and helpless women?"

"Are you and Ty supposed to be the fragile child and helpless woman in this scenario?" he asked as he pulled out his phone, "because I am calling Fyndham who, because of you, I now have as a contact in my phone. And if I were you I would come up with a different persona because he's not going to buy fragile and helpless."

"Hmmm, well I'll take that as a compliment," I stated as I stood up.

Hitch rolled his eyes and turned his back on us as he explained to Fyndham that there seemed to be human remains in a bag in the belfry. Detective Fyndham had worked on the case a few weeks ago when I had stumbled upon a dead guy in the parlor at the shelter, lying uh, next to the other dead guy. One was supposed to be dead and in the parlor because he had previously owned the mansion-cum-shelter. Evidently, his family had been "laid out" in that parlor for several generations. The other died as he was saying his final farewells to his friend. As it turned out, both of them had been murdered. Ezzie, my best friend, Mavis, Hitch, and I saw a lot of Fyndham while he was looking into that case. After it was closed, Ezzie and Fyndham, who she had nicknamed *Officer Handcuffs*, had started seeing a lot of each other in a nonprofessional capacity.

The three of us stood and took in the view for a few minutes in silence. It was breathtaking. You could see Stillwater and all its steeples and the St. Croix River beyond that. I didn't know much about forensics beyond what I learned on *CSI,* but I thought this was probably no big deal since those bones were old and dried out. I mean it was a big deal to whoever used to be attached to the bones, and probably their family, but most likely not an urgent case or anything. I hoped.

A few minutes later Fyndham and Ezzie came out the door onto the Belfry. Hitch raised one eyebrow when he saw Ez, clearly surprised that Fyndham had brought her along.

Before he could say anything Fyndham said, "We were together when the call came in and she had already gotten a text from Vivi and. . ."

Hitch just put a hand up to stop him with a look somewhere between, "I get it" and "I feel your pain."

Fyndham put on a pair of black latex gloves and thoroughly examined the bag. "Where was it when you found it?" he asked.

"Right there," I answered. "We didn't move it at all, just unzipped it."

"Why?" he asked.

"Why what?" I answered.

"Why did you unzip the bag?"

"Really? Why wouldn't I unzip the bag? I bet if I hadn't and just told someone it was up here you would be saying, 'Why didn't you look in the bag Miss Luxe? You seem to be suffering from an interesting lack of curiosity; perhaps you already knew what would be in there. DID YOU KNOW THERE WOULD BE BONES IN THERE?'"

I realized I might have gone too far lowering my voice and imitating the way he was standing because Ezzie was biting her lip trying not to laugh. Ty was big-eyed, and looked freaked out, while Hitch was shaking his head, AND rubbing his neck.

Fyndham didn't even blink. "Whose blood is this?" he asked, pointing to the stain that was now dark and dry.

"How do you know it was blood?" I asked. "What?" I asked again, turning towards Hitch seeing the look of disbelief and anger on his face. "Okay, okay, it's my blood. I scraped my elbow on the wall when I tripped over the bag. I wasn't evading the question, but come on, it's just a dark stain, I was interested to know how he knew it was blood."

"Ty, did you touch the bag too?" Fyndham asked.

"Yes, I did sir," Ty said quietly.

"Now that's how you answer a question," Hitch mumbled.

"Everyone can go. I've called a team; I'll wait for them to come up and sweep for prints and DNA. The bag looks fairly new, it hasn't seen any weather, so I would guess it's been up here less than a month. We have all your prints on file from the Kramer-

Anderson case, but I'll need Ty's to. . ."

"Why?" I asked.

"Why what, Vivi?" Fyndham asked.

"Why do you still have our prints? Why do our prints need to stay on file? We're not criminals. I don't want my prints in the system, that doesn't seem necessary. Ty hasn't done anything wrong, he shouldn't have to be printed."

"It's okay Vivi," Ty whispered to me. "Please don't argue with him."

I looked at Ty. His eyes were filling up with tears, and he was obviously terrified.

"Ty, you stand here and we'll get that picture," Hitch said, changing the subject. "How many more do you need?"

"Just two," he said, "but mine are so cool I could probably win without taking anymore."

"Good, let's get this one then you can take off." Hitch looked at Fyndham, who gave a slight head nod.

We all moved out of the shot. Hitch snapped the picture, and Ty ran out of the belfry like it was on fire.

"I'll need a list of who's been up here in the last eight weeks. My guess is there won't be any prints or DNA that's not tied to Vivi and Ty. I'll try to leave him out of it." Fyndham said.

"I should hope so," I said indignantly. "What is the matter with you, couldn't you see you were terrifying him for no reason?"

"Vivianna, you were the one scaring Ty," Hitch said quietly.

"You better have a heart to heart with your girl," Fyndham said to Hitch.

"With his gir. . ."

"Leave it," Hitch growled, cutting me off. "Have Mavis clean that arm up and put a bandage on it before you drip on another crime scene."

Hitch can be a little dramatic at times, I thought to myself. Ezzie decided she was going to stay with me at the shelter, so we headed to the main office to fill Mavis in on our morning.

*****

"Oh, fer the love. . ." Mavis said, shaking her head when we told her what happened. "How in the heck did those get up there? I have to be here all day, but I'll swing by for supper and let you know if I hear anything. You might as well go down to room 5B and grab the whiteboard."

Ezzie and I headed down the hall to retrieve the same whiteboard we had just recently returned there. We had used it as a crime board when we were trying to figure out the Kramer-Anderson murders. It had been useful, sort of, I guess. The truth was we were three amateur busybodies who had no idea what we were doing but had somehow figured out who had murdered two parishioners anyway. At least it was a place to put all of our thoughts. There had been one small hiccup when Hitch had seen his name on it with *"eat butt"* written after it. I had quickly explained that Ezzie had done a poor job of erasing, and it had originally said *"great butt"* which was, frankly, only slightly less horrifying to explain.

Kelli and the two little "Ks" were in the kitchen when we came through the back door and she asked, "Oh, what's the flip board for?"

Ezzie, always quick on her feet, said, "I'm working on a

project and need Vivi's help."

"Cool," Kelli said, "Where are you putting it?"

We stopped and looked at each other, then at the board. It was at least six feet wide and probably more than that tall. The last time we used it we had put it in the dining room and then the parlor. But now the house had way more people. Hitch would blow a gasket if the families saw it and got involved in our nonsense. Then again, Ty was in the middle of it and there was no way he wasn't going to tell Shayna and the older Ks about it.

"I guess we'll put it in the parlor for now," I said. "We can move it after lunch." The parlor was more formal than the den or the living room, the rooms where everyone usually hung out to watch TV or play games. It also had a heavy, intricately carved, nine-foot, solid cherry pocket door that we could slide shut.

It was Ashlee's day off, so she and Tootsie were home for lunch too. Ashlee was a tiny strawberry blonde mom. She had only recently turned eighteen and Tootsie, yes that was her real name, was six months old.

The lunch squad had set everything up in the kitchen. They were preparing a huge strawberry spinach salad with crusty bread for the adults and a variety of fruit, goldfish, cheese, and veggie sticks for the three and under set.

"Hey Kelli, I need to put you all on the board. Can I do that while we're waiting?" I asked, going over to the pantry door.

"Sure, what do you need?"

I explained that "The Board" was a chalkboard on the back of the pantry door. It was a way to keep track of our guests. It listed the parent's names, kids' names plus a little gender symbol, what room they were in, cell phone numbers, any approved guests, family schedules, and other notes, all in three neat columns.

She gave me her and Keith's cell phone numbers and his parents' names and numbers because they were approved guests. Then she added, "Kevin is twelve, Kandy is ten, Kraig is nine, Klark is five, Kristopher is three, and Kola is eighteen months."

I could see Ez's eyes get big as she pulled her lips tight in an impressive bout of self-control to keep from commenting. Earlier she had said, "Kandy, Kraig, and Klark are a stretch in my opinion, but Kola? They just gave up on real names altogether and started naming their kids after any word starting with a hard C." Poor little Kola. Did parents ever think about what their desire to be unique was doing to their kids' lives?

The front doorbell rang, so I excused myself from the table to get it. A pretty woman, probably in her mid to late fifties, well dressed with perfect makeup and hair, had a dozen dress bags hanging over her arm.

"Hi I'm donating these to the shelter," she said with a self-congratulatory grin. "It's formal wear that's been dry cleaned. I wanted it to go to our poor people, not just anybody because they are extraordinarily nice pieces, so you can understand that I didn't want to bring it to Goodwill."

"Uh, sure," I said, "But we have the GIV Clothing store, are you sure..."

"Yes!" she barked, her face contorting in anger at my stupidity. "I want it to go to good, poor people."

"Oh, okay, thank you," I said, thinking, *yeesh, arguing with her is way above my pay grade.*

Having satisfactorily given me her precious goods, she re-arranged her features so they returned to looking like the calm, cool woman who was standing on the porch when I initially opened the door.

"I'd like a tax credit slip please," she added.

"You will need to call the main office for that, we don't have them here," I said as she spun on her heel and left before my sentence was even finished. She looked over her shoulder at me and said, "No I don't suppose you would."

What was that supposed to mean? I wondered. I felt insulted but couldn't say why. I brought the bags back into the kitchen with me and showed Ashlee, Kelli, and Ez.

"Oooh, Nordstrom's," Ez said, looking at the bags.

We started opening them. The first dress was a long beige beaded column dress. Very plain, non-offensive, but kind of old ladyish.

"Looks like a dress a mother of a groom would wear," Kelli said, rather astutely.

The next was almost identical but in a dull bruise color that was kind of a horrid, dark faded-plum. The third bag had a sleeveless, straight, long brown lace dress with an empire waist and a knee-length flowy cover-up. The fourth was a silk taupe-on-beige horizontal striped, ruched nightmare, for which there were hardly words.

"Yikes, it's like a slug crawled away and left its pale carcass behind," Ez said, wrinkling her nose. Apparently there were words.

"Yep, Old lady gala dresses," I said as I unzipped the next bag. They were all long, moderately expensive, although clearly off the rack and fairly nondescript.

"Yeah, a gala for people in witness protection where no one wants to stand out," Ezzie said.

"Why would anyone think that we needed party dresses if we're living at a shelter?" Kelli asked.

"Why would anyone think you needed ugly party dresses no matter where you lived?" Ezzie added logically.

"Maybe if we cut them off?" Ashlee said.

"Maybe," I said, doubtfully.

"At the neckline," Ez added.

We decided the girls probably wouldn't even want to play dress-up in them because the colors were so depressing. I walked the bags over to the clothing store, and the staff and volunteers just shook their heads and groaned. I walked past the Fellowship Hall where the older kids were watching a slideshow of their pictorial scavenger hunt. *Wow, impressive,* I thought. *Someone must have spent their lunch break pulling this all together.* There was a tally board and Ty was tied for first place. Good for him; he needed a win.

When I got back, Ez and I sat outside sipping on some super-secret *"Seniorita Bajo en Calorias Margaritas,"* our favorite margarita mix. We weren't supposed to have alcohol at the shelter when there were families around, but I had just found a bag of bones so decided I'd break the rules this once. We filled our Yeti's with ice and headed out to Ezzie's car because she had a magnum of it in her trunk. Then we slunk our way into the lounge chairs in the backyard feeling like we were sneaking booze out of our parents' liquor cabinet in high school. We sat out in the sun talking until Hitch and Mavis came across the lawn.

"What's for supper?" Hitch asked.

"Menu board said bacon-wrapped asparagus, chopped sirloin, Caprese salad, and ciabatta," I said. "The Food Squad fired up the grill about twenty minutes ago so it won't be long."

The shelter had eight teams of cooks called the "Food Squads." They volunteered on a rotating schedule to prepare meals at the shelter. Terri was the Food Squad Coordinator and made sure everything was running smoothly. Each Food Squad had six people, and they all seemed to do their weeks differently. This week all six came for breakfast, then came back for lunch, and then all six returned to make dinner. Mavis said they were retired and probably a little bored, so couldn't wait for their week to feel useful. Mavis seemed to have the ability to tap into everyone's boredom and need to feel useful because she had groups that volunteered to do just about everything at Grace in the Valley.

Ty and Shayna burst through the kitchen door a few steps ahead of their mother, just as dinner was being served. "Vivi look," he said running up to me, shoving a new, cool-looking camera towards me. "It's a Canon."

"I see," I said.

"I won it, I didn't steal it," he said.

"Of course you didn't steal it," I said, shocked that he would even think to say such a thing,

"Congrats man. You must have won the photo contest today," Hitch chimed in.

"Yeah. I was tied all day with this Sydney girl, but I think the bell picture put me ahead."

"That's awesome," Ezzie added.

We all looked at the camera, passed it around, and the Food Squad promised a congratulatory dessert. Everyone moved into the dining room for supper. All six of the K-kids gobbled up every single bite on their plates, including the asparagus and the tomatoes. Even baby Kola. I was shocked and impressed. The Food Squad put a candle in the center of a four-layer chocolate cake for Ty, and we sang "Congratulations to you" to the tune of Happy Birthday.

The families said they would have some later, but Mavis, Ezzie, Hitch and I took our cake out to the front porch, a ritual we enjoyed several times a week. It was another gorgeous night. GIV was far enough away from the city that the stars seemed close and the air was sweet.

"Do you think Ty should talk to someone?" I asked no one in particular.

"We'll probably have Sherry talk to him a few times. He already knows her and feels comfortable," Hitch answered knowing exactly what I was getting at.

Sherry was one of the caseworkers at GIV Community Center and worked with Shawna, Shayna, and Ty.

"Vivi, do you know why Ty was so freaked out today?" Hitch asked.

"Well, I assume it was finding a bag of human remains," I answered.

"Yes, that was part of it, but I think the main reason was how you were talking to Fyndham."

"Jake's a big boy," Ezzie interjected. "I talk to him like that all the time."

"Officer Handcuff's name is Jake?" I said. "Shoot, I was really hoping it was Willy because Willy Find-em is hilarious."

"Ha, thank God it's not, even if he pronounces it finned-um, still too close," Ezzie giggled.

"Yes, well hilarity aside," Hitch broke in, "Ty was afraid for you, Vivi. I'm sure his mom has had *the talk* with him."

"*The talk?*" I repeated.

"If you're a young black male your parent or parents sit you down and make sure you clearly understand that you keep your hands in plain view and talk with extreme politeness to all police officers under all circumstances."

"Well yeah," I replied. "I mean my dad told me the same thing. If you get pulled over, turn the inside light on in the car, keep your hands on the wheel and answer politely. But I mean it was Fyndham, Ezzie's new boy, errr, acquaintance fellow." I looked at Ezzie stumbling over the words. I had never known her to go out with anyone more than two or three times except Stephen and didn't know what to call him.

Stephen is Ezzie's "probably husband."Their families have known each other forever. Stephen proposed to Ezzie and she accepted. When she was six. As adults they have an agreement to date whomever they want as long as they keep it in the back of their minds that they'll get married someday. He's a partner at a law firm in Boston, and they see each other about three times a year. Ezzie's dates, to date, have always been casual, but I can tell she likes Fyndham.

"Why," Hitch said.

"Why what?" I asked.

"Why do you think your dad told you to put your hands on the steering wheel and talk politely to officers if you got pulled over?"

"Because he knew I tended to be, um chatty?" I offered.

"And?" he asked.

"And he didn't want me to make matters worse," I admitted.

"Or?" Hitch prodded.

"You know I hate when you do this, don't you," I said. Ezzie and Mavis just sat and silently watched the two of us.

"Or?" Hitch repeated not giving an inch.

"Or I guess I could end up getting a ticket, be arrested, get a bigger fine," I sighed.

"Yeah Viv, Shawna told Ty that because he could end up dead," Hitch said.

I just sat there and looked at him. I mean, I guess I knew that black males had a bigger chance of getting picked up or getting caught up in police violence, but not fourteen-year-olds. "But that happens to like gang bangers, not sweet kids like Ty," I said.

"Vivi, Ty is very attached to you, as is Shayna. I know that we have one black family and two white families right now, but that's not the norm. We will be helping more families of color at the shelter. You are going to start to love these kids, and they will love you back. Do some homework," Hitch said.

CHAPTER 2

Wednesday

I went downstairs, and the Food Squad was there making waffles to order. Ezzie and I decided we were eating in the upstairs lounge so I grabbed a big tray. While I poured juice and picked out fruit and bacon, they made us fresh waffles. I grabbed a bowl with whipped cream, a small pitcher of syrup, plates, silverware, and napkins. Shawna was walking into the kitchen as I was headed upstairs.

"Shawna, I'm so sorry that Ty was anywhere near that bag yesterday. Is he okay?" I asked.

"I think so. Winning the camera helped. I didn't know white people spent so much time dealing with dead bodies."

"Yeah, if it's any consolation there wasn't actually a body this time, just bones."

We were just finishing breakfast when we heard Mavis calling us from downstairs. Ashlee and Tootsie had been up and out since six o'clock. Ashlee was a CNA at a local long-term care facility, and they had daycare on site which was convenient for her. The problem was once she paid for daycare on a CNA salary, there was not much left over for rent.

Keith was doing a temporary construction job with his brother-in-law, Kelli and the little Ks were at the Resource Center, and the older Ks were with Ty and Shayna at art camp. Shawna was at work, so the house was empty.

"I thought you girls might have brought the flip-board upstairs to your lounge," Mavis said.

"It was too big to get up the stairs," I admitted.

"Oh well, keeping that door shut is a good idea in case Pastor Nosy-Pants comes by," she said. "I brought a list of everyone who has used the bell tower going twelve weeks back. Of course, those are the ones who asked to use it. Anyone with a master key can get up there anytime."

"How many master keys are there?" I asked.

"Oh, about a hundred G-master keys, but this is an S-master."

"What's the difference?" Ez asked before I could.

"The G is for General," Mavis explained. "All staff members have one. It gets them into classrooms, closets, and the kitchen. The S is for supervisors and it gets them into Finance offices, Pastor Hitch's office, the belfry, the Pipe Room, and the Tech Room."

"Okay, so how many S-keys?" I asked, thinking I didn't need all the G-key info, but there was no stopping Mavis when she was on a roll.

"About fifteen I think," she said. "I brought pictures of almost everyone, and I'm still looking for a picture of the MoGOs. I'm going to find a group shot of them."

I wasn't sure I wanted to know but asked anyway, "Who are the MoGOs?"

"That's our moms' group, it's an acronym for Moms Getting Out. They're a group that meets every Thursday. Their kids go to the nursery which gives them two hours to talk to other grownups. They have a different topic every week, everything from politics to investing."

"And they have an S-key?" I asked

"No, no key at all, but they had their group meeting up in the bell tower about three weeks ago."

"Why?" Ez and I asked at the same time.

"Beth, their leader, asked William if he would take them up there and tell them about the bell then he brought them into the Pipe Room."

Sometimes the more Mavis explained things the more confused I became. "Okay, Mavis. Who is William, what's the Pipe Room, and what's so interesting about the bell?"

"William Jackdaw is our organist. The Pipe Room is where all the pipes are for the pipe organ; it's quite impressive. The bell was a gift from a French church. William knows all the details and it's a great tour."

"Well obviously if there was a group of them, the bones had to have been brought up there after they did their tour," I reasoned.

"How heavy is a bag of bones anyway?" Ez asked. "I think if we knew that, we could narrow things down a bit."

"That's a good point Ez. We're getting good at this," I said.

Mavis poked her head out the door and yelled towards the kitchen, "Alexa, how much does a skeleton weigh?"

We ran into the kitchen to hear Alexa saying, "The average human skeleton will account for approximately fourteen percent of total body weight. Going by the average American male over the age of twenty weighing two hundred pounds, the skeletal weight will be twenty-seven point five pounds. The average female skeleton will weigh twenty-three pounds."

"Can we go up there again?" I asked Mavis. "I'm going to grab some sugar and flour and see if I can carry it up the steps."

We went into the kitchen and realized we only had half a five-pound bag of sugar and an almost empty ten-pound bag of flour.

"Well let's go to the church kitchen," Mavis suggested. "They have bigger quantities."

*****

We found a fifty-pound bag of rice and dumped half of it in a bin. Then we taped up the bag and headed for the bell tower. It was kind of grueling I thought, but I made it to the top with the rice.

"Well I can do it," I said, leaning against the wall, trying to catch my breath.

"Huh, that doesn't narrow things down much," Ez said.

We took a moment to enjoy the breeze and the scenery. Ezzie agreed to carry the rice down for me. I opened the door holding it by the edge. My hand was over the latch and when I pulled it away there was a sticky residue left on my hand.

"Hey, look at this," I said, squatting down to look at the door. "It's sticky."

"Like someone put tape over the latch," Mavis said, looking more closely.

We stood there staring at it for a minute and Ez finally said, "Well now we know it has to be someone who can carry about twenty-five pounds of rice up all these steps and that they taped the latch open."

"Or someone who knew it was taped open," I added. Not sure if it made the suspect list longer or shorter.

"Well, fiddle-sticks," was all Mavis said.

"So, are we going to try to figure this one out too?" Ez asked.

"We're pretty good at it," I said. "And we did roll the flip board over to the house already."

"And I've worked here a long time, "Mavis added. "I feel like I should know who's messing with the church. It just isn't right."

With that decision made, Ez headed back to the house, and I followed Mavis to the kitchen to put the rice back. Mavis went back to work and I headed home. When I stepped out the door to go back to the shelter I had to jump back as a motorcycle roared past me almost running over my toes and, more importantly, my sunflower yellow strappy Jimmy Choo's.

The maniac parked his bike next to Hitch's Harley, took off his helmet, swung his long leg over the bike, and walked towards me. I was ready to blast into him, but the closer he got, the cuter he was. He had brown hair, light grey eyes, a little bit of a crooked smile, and two huge dimples.

"I don't know what you're smiling at," I snapped. "You almost killed me."

"Well you can't blame me for that," he said, the smile getting wider and the dimples getting deeper. "I was driving along minding my own business, and the most beautiful woman I've ever seen stepped right in front of me. I'm lucky my heart didn't stop."

"Mmm hmm," I said, the flattery working despite my attempt at staying angry.

"What are you doing alone in the church parking lot, besides seducing unsuspecting motorists?" he asked.

"I work here. What caused you to race in here like a bat out of hell?"

"I'm dropping off a check for my mother. She forgot it at home on Sunday and doesn't want the church to think she is a bad parishioner."

"Well, that's kind of sweet; you're a good son."

"Not that good, I was supposed to do it three weeks ago. Shhh, don't tell anyone."

"Oh man, you are in trouble now. The treasurer makes a call after two weeks of non-giving, so the gig is up," I said, shaking my head and trying to look dire.

"Really?" he asked, squinting his eyes in disbelief.

"No, not really," I admitted. I was still a little uncertain about the whole lying on church property and the resulting effects it had in regards to one's eternity, so I figured I better let him off the hook.

"Well that's a relief," he said laughing. "What do you do here at the church?"

"I'm the House Mother at the shelter," I said nodding at the mansion across the parking lot.

"House Mother?" he said, raising an eyebrow.

"It's more of an administrative role," I quickly added. I got a muddled image in my mind every time I heard the term house mother. I wasn't sure what a house mother was, but I knew the words, 'old,' 'boring,' and 'spinster' came to mind. Observing the reactions of others when I said the term, I could only assume they had thoughts along the same lines.

"Well are you allowed to leave the church property?" he asked.

"Why do you want to know?"

"I was wondering if you would like to have dinner with me tomorrow evening?"

"I don't even know your name, dinner seems like a big step."

"It's Chad," he said, reaching a hand out for me to shake. "Chad Everest."

"Hello Chad Everest, I'm Vivianna Luxe."

"So Vivianna, how about dinner?"

"That would be great," I agreed, surprising myself.

"I'll pick you up at six tomorrow. Pazzaluna in St. Paul okay?"

"Perfect, I've heard great things," I said, as I sauntered away from him across the parking lot.

Hitch and Mavis came over a few minutes later. The lunch team had made tomato soup, grilled cheese and sliced apples with a yogurt dipping sauce. Ez and I had been amazed and delighted by the tomato soup and grilled cheese combination a few weeks before. Both of us had grown up with live-in cooks, and the closest thing we had to grilled cheese when we were young was a crostini or possibly bruschetta. Mavis chuckled and Hitch just shook his head as we marveled over this delicious combo all over again.

"Hey, Chad Everest asked me to dinner," I said. "He's not an ax murderer is he?"

"Chad Everett?" Mavis and Hitch said at the same time.

"No, Everest," I corrected, wondering why Mavis looked disappointed and Hitch was smirky.

"What?" I asked, knowing they had something to say.

"Chad Everett was a hunky doctor on the *Marcus Welby* show," Mavis said. "Dr. Rich Gannon."

"Joe," Hitch corrected.

"Joe who?" I asked.

"Joe Gannon, Rich Gannon was a quarterback for the Vikings."

"Oh yes, of course," Mavis agreed. "Say, didn't he marry someone's daughter?"

"Bill Brown," Hitch answered.

"The guy who sang, *I Feel Good*?" Ezzie asked.

"No, that's Jim Brown, this is Boom-Boom Brown, a former Minnesota Vik. . ."

"Enough!" I interrupted, "As fascinating as Boom-Boom Everett is, does anyone know anything about Chad Everest? He dropped off a check for his mom today."

"Oh sure, Lilian's boy. She's delightful; I don't know Chad. The check was dated three weeks ago if that tells you anything," Mavis said.

"Where did you meet Chad?" Ez asked.

"In the parking lot after I dropped off the rice," I answered.

"Maybe I'll start hanging out in the parking lot; you get a lot of action out there."

I had met Doug Jacobson in the parking lot a few weeks earlier. He asked me out before he had to leave to work on a design project in Austin, Texas. He owned a design and consulting firm. Unfortunately, I missed our date because I was in the hospital after the whole getting pushed down the stairs incident.

"The church parking lot is not there as a meat market for you two," Hitch said without much humor. "Does this guy know it's not the Jurassic period?"

"Ha-ha," I said, rolling my eyes at him. I had recently been picked up at a funeral by a cute surfer-looking guy named Arthur Gottfried. He had thought dinosaurs were still roaming the earth, among some other not so bright ideas. He had been a total nightmare, and Hitch had to come and rescue me from a street dance when I couldn't take one more minute of his nit-wittedness.

Hitch headed back to church after lunch and Mavis, Ezzie,

and I headed into the parlor. Mavis handed us five pictures to put on the board.

"Mavis, this is Hitch," I stated. This seemed a little unnecessary, but I wasn't an expert on crime-solving so who was I to say what was and wasn't a waste of space.

"Isn't this just a waste of space?"

"We're being thorough," she said and handed out the rest of the pictures.

"That's Mark, he's the night custodian. His brother Mitch works during the day. They both have keys, but Mark was up there sweeping after that bad storm a couple of weeks ago."

"At night? That seems weird," I said.

"As soon as the rain stopped, he went up there."

"Oh, I recognize this guy," Ez said, taping a picture up of a nice-looking man with brown hair and kind brown eyes. "He's the organist, right?"

"Yes. That's William Jackdaw." Mavis said, "And this is Deacon Lila." She added a picture of a pretty blonde woman wearing a pastor's robe. She looked to be in her mid twenties.

"And who's in the last picture?" I asked.

"It's a group photo of the MoGOs," Mavis said. "They meet on Thursdays. I think you should go over there tomorrow and see what kind of vibe you get off of them."

"To a moms' group? What would I possibly say?" I asked.

"Well, tell them you're the new housemother at the shelter and even though your role as a mother isn't traditional, you feel like you want some insight and support."

"That's pretty good," Ez said with admiration in her voice.

"And then what, look for the person who's wearing a skull

and crossbones T-shirt that says, *I did it*?"

"Well that would be convenient," Mavis said, "but just see what you think about them. I know them all pretty well so it will be good to have fresh eyes."

"Oh brother. What do I wear, like mom jeans?" I asked.

"Oh no, they're really fashionable, but casual you know," Mavis said.

Not really, I thought. What the heck was I going to do in a mom's group. I wasn't a very good liar; someone was bound to figure out that I was snooping. The landline started ringing as I was mulling over this MoGO idea.

"GIV Family Shelter," Ez said, answering the extension sitting on a little phone table in the parlor. "Mmm hmm, uh-huh, yes, she'll be right over." She hung up and turned to me, "Mrs. Schmidt says you need to come over to pick up Ty; she didn't sound happy."

"Oh, fer lands-sake," Mavis said.

"Well shit," I said at the same time.

Mrs. Schmidt ran the summer camp program. There were separate directors for preschool, grade school, middle school, and high school. She oversaw all of them. They all had the same theme each week but ran age-appropriate activities.

A few weeks back Ty had super-glued some quarters to the floor and the bathroom faucets. He hid and watched kids try to pick them up and guys get squirted when they turned on the faucet. Mrs. Schmidt had been furious. I had suggested it was immature but kind of a funny harmless prank. She suggested I was immature and kicked Ty out anyway. Hitch had pulled rank and reinstated him in time for Ty to see a "totally tight" Christian rapper and be part of cutting a CD in an actual recording studio. I assumed Mrs. Schmidt didn't like that, and I had been waiting for the other shoe to drop. Looks like the time had come.

*****

"Ty was in a bus seat on the way to the art museum and scaring children who would sit down," Mrs. Schmidt said to me when I got to her office.

"I can't imagine Ty purposefully scaring anyone," I said.

"Oh, it was purposeful," she said.

"So where were the kids he was scaring?" I asked, trying to figure out what exactly had happened.

"They were in the seat," Mrs. Schmidt said.

"With Ty?"

"Of course, that's why they got scared."

"I'm sorry," I said, "but what did he do that scared them?"

"He moved or made a noise of course," she said.

I was starting to get angry because none of this made any sense. "All the kids are high schoolers, so if they chose to sit with Ty how scared could they be if he moved or made a noise? You can't expect him to be stick-still and silent the entire way to the art museum."

"He was in the seat," Mrs. Schmidt said with more insistence.

"Yes, I heard you. I assume all kids were supposed to be in their seats."

She drew in a long breath and then exhaled. "Miss Luxe, he was IN the seat," she said huffily.

I just sat there looking at her feeling like we were speaking different languages.

"The back of the seat was pulled open and Ty crawled inside the seat, then when children sat down he would move or make a noise and he would scare them," she said.

I was finally getting a visual of what happened. I could picture kids sitting in the bus seat and all of a sudden it moved or talked to them. I started laughing and had to bend at the waist with tears running down my face.

"Oh, come on," I said, "this might be the funniest thing I've ever heard."

"So you said about the last vandalism incident. Perhaps you think terrifying children is funny. I do not."

"Okay, first of all, these are high schoolers, not kinder-garteners. And they were startled, not terrified. I think we can lighten up just a bit, don't you?"

"Miss Luxe, I do not need to debate this with you. Are you going to take Ty with you or do I need to call his mother at work and the police?"

"Good grief lady, I'll take Ty with me, but I have serious reservations about the appropriateness of you being around kids. Or humans. You should be ashamed of yourself."

"I think. . ."

"Frankly my dear, I don't give a damn what you think," I said cutting her off, throwing in a little Rhett for good measure, and slamming the door as I exited.

"Come on Ty," I said, grabbing him from outside her office. We walked home in silence. That woman made me want to kick something.

Ty and I were sitting in the kitchen eating leftover choc-olate cake, not talking. Mavis came over a few minutes later and said, "Here's the church credit card. As long as you two aren't busy for the rest of the day, can you go get decorations and fun stuff for the 4th?"

"Sure," I said. "How much should I spend?"

"Oh, about fifty or sixty bucks I guess," Mavis said. "Go to the dollar store."

"I love the dollar store," Ty said.

I had never been to a dollar store. In my former life, I was more of a Nordstrom's, Bergdorf's or high-end boutique kind of girl. I realized I hadn't been into any store since Daddy had been forced out of the country and all the money was gone. This could be fun I decided.

*****

We wandered up and down the aisles with a cart. It was the most amazing thing I had ever seen. You could get almost anything for a dollar. We got packs of glow sticks, red, white, and blue plastic cups, mason jar glasses with flags on them, striped plates, red, white, and blue pennant banners and bunting, and eight pairs of various sized red and white flip flops with navy blue sequins on the straps. I grabbed a few red, white and blue boas right at the end for the girls and some boingy-star headbands. Then as we waited in line I spotted citronella candles in pails decorated with stars and stripes and sparklers, so I grabbed those too. It all came to sixty-five dollars which I figured was in the ballpark.

It was fun piling all the bags in the back of my car. I hadn't been on a shopping spree in ages. We decided we should put the top up so nothing flew out. I had a 1971 Cuda convertible. Daddy had given it to me when I turned twenty-one. He decided against the more traditional 'sassy green' or 'curious yellow' and had the paint color matched to my eyes. It was kind of a misty, forest-green with a white ragtop and white leather interior. It was my summer car. In the winter I put it in the garage and drove a black Lamborghini Urus. Well, in past winters. In hindsight that might have been the more practical vehicle to take when I escaped to my new life, but it was only worth a fraction of what the Cuda was worth, and I really, really loved this car.

Ezzie had found the bus seat story as funny as I did. Shawna, Ty's mom, did not. It was a quiet supper, and all the Ks darted off to the den to play games and watch TV as fast as they could.

"Shawna, if it's any consolation, I think Mrs. Schmidt is not being fair to Ty," I said, as we carried our plates from the dining room to the kitchen.

"It doesn't matter," she said. "I try to explain to him that you need to 'play the game.' Even if someone is being unfair, that's how life goes and you have to learn to deal with those people."

"I'm sorry," I said, not knowing what else to say. "It seems hard to grow from a boy to a man. Little girls are kind of who they are going to be only smaller, but boys have to go from sweet funny little toddlers to big strong men with all sorts of societal expectations and unwritten rules in between."

Shawna looked at me and burst into tears. "Thank you for saying that. Sometimes I just get so tired."

We stood in the kitchen and hugged it out. She was such a good mom and worked so hard at her two jobs. I could feel her exhaustion, worry, and fear.

*****

At nine o'clock I went over to the church to talk to Mark, the night janitor. Mavis had given me her S-key. I tried to listen to see if I could hear a vacuum or music from a radio, but the whole place was as dark and silent as a tomb. I knew he was here because his truck was in the lot.

I poked my head into the sanctuary and could see a light at the front coming from the little room area that was behind the altar. I headed down the side aisle thinking he must be back there cleaning. When I was about halfway down the aisle I realized I hadn't rehearsed what I was going to say. "Hey fella, did you drag a bag of bones up to the belfry?" seemed wrong. "Did you see a bag of bones in the belfry and not mention it?" seemed equally bad. I decided this whole thing was a fool's errand. I turned around to leave and a huge hand grabbed my shoulder.

"Whaaaa!" I screamed my heart leaping to my throat.

"How'd you get in here?" a voice about a foot above the hand growled.

"I have Mavis' key," I squeaked.

The voice didn't say more but didn't let go of my shoulder either.

"Are you Mark?" I asked.

"Why?" he asked back.

"Um, I was just, well sort of, wondering, if you saw anything in the bell tower that would explain why there was a bag of bones up there."

"No," was all he said.

"Okay, thank you very much, I'll just be running back to the shelter then. Where I work. And where there are so many people waiting for me. Ha, probably with their phones out ready to call 911 if I'm not back soon, really soon, they're such worry-warts. For no good reason, of course, nothing to worry about here. I mean I'm not worried, but, you know there are a bunch of little kids, and they need me, and they worry," I babbled.

He finally let go of my shoulder, and I bolted up the aisle towards the sanctuary entrance. I stepped outside into the warm night air and someone grabbed my arm.

"Mother Fu. . ."

"Vivi, it's me," Hitch said, interrupting my queen mother of all curses. "What are you doing here?"

"What am I doing here?" I said, my terror slowly subsiding. "I work here, what are you doing here?"

"Yes well, if memory serves, I am the lead pastor here, so I work here too," he added, less than amused.

"Well, carry on," I said, attempting to walk away.

Hitch pulled me back into his chest and grabbed my other arm as well. Then he leaned down and whispered in my ear in a most disturbing way, "If I find out you were messing around in the bell tower, we are going to have a serious problem."

Knowing that Hitch had spent time in prison before becoming a pastor was probably what was making my knees weak, and having had two frights in less than two minutes was definitely why my heart was pounding, I told myself. It had nothing to do with his lips being so close to my ear.

"Well I wasn't up there," I squeaked, "and just so you know, your night custodian is scary as hell," I added.

"Well yes, there's a reason he works nights with no people around," Hitch said, releasing his grip. I scurried off to the shelter the second he let me go.

CHAPTER 3

Thursday

I was sitting in a circle of chairs in one of the larger meeting rooms with thirteen women who were busy chatting with each other. Mavis was right, they were all well-dressed. I had gone with a Ralph Lauren wide-striped cotton blouse with a widespread collar. The blue and white stripes seemed fitting since the 4th was right around the corner. The white Piazza Sempione Brigette capri's were perfect with it. I loved this outfit. It was what Ez and I called a "kidnap" outfit, something you wouldn't mind wearing day after day if you got kidnapped. My Dolce & Gabbana blue leather slide sandals were the exact color of the blue in the blouse, and I could wear them forever because they were so comfortable. Worth every penny of the nine-hundred-dollar price tag. The shirt and pants had been just over five hundred dollars each so the whole outfit was kind of a bargain. Oh yeah, ever since Daddy left with all the money, I had started the irritating habit of keeping a running total of every article of clothing I put on, which was ironic because I had never paid attention to the price of anything before a month ago.

We had been invited to have a "treat" before we took our seats. I was told everyone took turns bringing something. A woman named Kendra had told me that it had turned into somewhat of a competition. *This week it's Kelli Reese's turn, so I'm sure it will be amazing,* she had said. There was a chafing dish with Eggs Benedict. Kelli had made it with crab cakes instead of English muffins and the poached eggs were cupped in an avocado half. She brought compostable plates and silverware made from bamboo. The silverware was wrapped in a red and blue cloth napkin with a white star lily, from her garden, tied on each one with raffia. A folded table tent said, "Keep the napkin and flower, stars and stripes in honor of the 4th."

A rail-thin blonde woman called everyone to order and

said, "I see we have a visitor today. We will start with devotions and then go around and introduce ourselves. Please give your name, your husband's name, your kids' names and ages, and answer our question of the week which is, *what is the most exotic vacation you've ever taken in July?*"

"Devotions" I found out was what they called a feel-good spiritual reading from, oddly enough, a book about chicken soup. Apparently, everyone took turns and could read whatever they wanted. I thought it was interesting that the assumption was that everyone had a husband. Then it was more interesting that everyone except one timid young woman had one. When it was my turn, I repeated Mavis' excuse for my attendance, that I was the house mother for the shelter, and although not a mother in the traditional sense, I found I was looking for an outlet for adult conversation and a sympathetic ear.

"And what is your most exotic July vacation?" Beth the leader asked.

"When I was ten, my dad and I traveled around the world. My mom had just left us, and we used redecorating my bedroom as an excuse to get out of town so to speak," I said. "We bonded over learning the intricacies of Victorian antique boudoir furnishings, trying new foods, and seeing most of the seven modern wonders of the world."

"Really?" Beth said, in a way which could mean, 'wow that's lovely' or 'you're a big fat liar.' "Which ones did you miss?"

"Sadly, we didn't go to Jordan to see Petra," I said.

I listened as each of the women told about their trips. Beth had been to Kathmandu, and I thought she probably thought I had rained on her parade. As each woman spoke I couldn't help but notice their purses. Six of them had Birkin Bags, I saw two Tom Ford totes, a Valextra tote, a Gucci tote, and a Burberry tote. The young timid mom's name was Kristin Sells. She was darling with shaggy bangs and bright blue eyes but an unfortunate large nose. She said she had always worked summers, as had her mom while she was growing up, so the most exotic place she had gone in July was Valley Fair. I noticed she had an ordinary backpack sitting at her feet.

I stayed after the official meeting was over and tried to chat with each of the women for a bit. I didn't get any *bone vibes* off any of them, but I guess I hadn't expected that I would. I swung by the main office to fill Mavis in on how my two hours of impersonating a mom had gone.

"Oh, I'm so glad you're here. I need to run to the Post Office. Can you watch the phones for me? Our receptionist just left for a doctor's appointment."

"Um, I could just go to the Post Office," I said, sounding as panicky as I felt.

"No, I have to go. I have to re-register the postage machine. Come here, I'll show you what to do."

I walked around the desk and Mavis showed me the phone bank with the entire staff listed alphabetically by first name. If someone wanted somebody I just had to press transfer and then the corresponding button. If there were questions I didn't know, I was supposed to answer politely and say someone would call them back with an answer. It didn't sound too hard.

It was as if the universe sensed Mavis' departure. The second she stepped out the door the phone started ringing. "Hello, Grace in the Valley," I said. "Yes, one moment I'll transfer you." The first six or seven calls were all pretty straightforward, people asking for one staff member or another.

And then, "Can you help me get to Sun Ray please?" the woman on the other end of the line said.

"Excuse me," I said, "I'm not sure what you are asking."

"I'm in my car, and I just can't find Sun Ray Shopping

Center."

"Oh. Did you know you called a church?" I asked logically.

"Of course, I've been a member for fifty-seven years," the woman told me.

"Um, okay, so I'm not sure how I can help exactly?"

"Well I'm driving, I have no way to look up directions, and I'm trying to get to Sun Ray."

"Oh, um, uh, sure," I said, not sure at all. I pulled out my cell phone and Googled directions to Sun Ray Shopping Center.

"Can you tell me where you are right now?" I asked.

"I don't know, that's the problem," she replied.

"Well can you see any street signs?"

"Oh, good thinking," she said enthusiastically.

"Yes, I'm on McKnight and I just crossed Stillwater."

I played around with the map for a bit zooming in and out until I found the intersection she was talking about. I gave directions and listened to her recite the name of every crossroad as she passed them until I talked her into the Sun Ray parking lot. She thanked me profusely and hung up.

"What are you doing?" I heard Hitch ask from behind me.

"Mavis had to go to the post office, I'm taking the phone for her while she's gone," I answered.

"I can see that, but what was it you were just doing with the directions?"

"Some lady called, she's been a member for fifty years and couldn't find her way to Sun Ray," I told him. "That might be the oddest reason anyone has ever called a church."

"Not even close," he said, heading back to his office. "Mavis and I are coming over for lunch," he added over his shoulder. "The Food Squad is making homemade chicken noodle soup."

I would turn my chair so Hitch couldn't sneak up behind me if I was Mavis, but she'd been here forever so she must have a system for keeping track of him.

*****

When I got back home, Ez, Ty, Kelli, and the little Ks were there. I had asked Ezzie to come over because there were always supposed to be two adults with any minor child at the shelter. Then again technically we weren't supposed to be "babysitting" any of the kids at the shelter. A parent or approved person was always supposed to be with a minor child. But Ty was fourteen and Kelli had said she would be responsible for him while I was gone. EZ was just a bonus set of eyes.

The Food Squad had indeed made homemade chicken noodle soup, including homemade noodles. I was excited to try it because I hadn't had homemade noodles like this before. They were kind of rustic and thick and looked amazing.

Ez and I sat out on the back porch and waited for Mavis and Hitch. I told her that Hitch had caught me in the parking lot last night, and was bound to bring it up because he was not a "just let it slide" kind of guy.

"I could go forever pretending something didn't happen," Ez said.

"Agreed," I acknowledged.

Mavis and Hitch came across the lot and sat on the porch with us while we waited for lunch.

"I invited Jake for lunch," Ez said,

"Fyndham's coming for lunch?" Hitch said. He had a look on his face like he was processing how he felt about that.

"He said he had some info for you so I thought it would be polite," Ezzie added.

"Well sure, inviting someone to a home you don't live in, never-the-less seem to be in most of the time, seems like the mannerly thing to do," Hitch said.

"Exactly Padre," Ez retorted.

Fyndham came a few minutes later. Kelli and the little Ks had to leave to go pick up Keith so it was a good thing, Jake, Hitch, and Mavis had come over or the Food Squad would have been sad just feeding Ty and me.

"You have news," Hitch stated more than asked Jake.

Jake looked around the table at Ezzie, Ty, and me, and then must have decided we had all been in the belfry so we could hear the news. "Forensics confirmed the bag was new and hadn't been out in the weather more than six weeks, which we already guessed. If they had to narrow it down they would say seven to fourteen days. The remains in the bag were actually from two people. They were both in the system so it came back fast. They belong to Henry and Sharon Olson."

"What the heck."

"That's not possible."

Hitch and Mavis blurted at the same time.

"We just buried Henry Olson about nine months ago," Hitch continued, "and Sharon is very much alive. I saw her in church on Sunday."

"Well Olson is a fairly common name," Jake said, showing

no emotion at all. "Here's a picture from their driver's licenses," he said, handing the pictures to Hitch.

Mavis leaned over to see them, and she and Hitch looked at each other. "That's the same guy we buried, but his wife was in church Sunday. And those bones are not from a guy who only died nine months ago," Hitch said.

"Probably twenty years at least," Jake agreed.

We all sat in silence for a few seconds lost in the incongruence of what had just been said.

"Was there any useful DNA or fingerprints in the bell tower?" Mavis asked.

"Just two sets on the bag and the walls. One set is Vivi's and we're assuming the second set is Ty's. Sorry, Ty, we are going to have to get your prints to compare, but I'll do my best to keep them out of the system after that," Jake said.

Ty just nodded and looked a little freaked out.

"There wasn't even anything on the sticky stuff?" I asked. "I thought for sure that would have something." Oops. Yeah something like Mavis, Ez, and my fingerprints since we all touched it repeatedly.

"What sticky stuff?" Jake said.

Hitch was starting to do his scary squinty thing at me, but I soldiered on. "On the edge of the door, over the latch. Like it had been taped open."

I heard the smallest groan come from Hitch. "What? I was not up there last night," I said, trying to ward that conversation off.

"I don't know that anyone noticed that," Jake admitted. "When did you notice it, Vivianna?"

Uh-oh, full name. "Yesterday," I said, finally adopting the

less-is-more style of answering that usually abandoned me.

"And who was with you?" Hitch asked.

"I think detective Fyndham is perfectly capable of asking his own questions," I said, giving Hitch my own squinty evil eye.

"Vivi. . ." Hitch started in his menacing voice.

"Who else went up there with you?" Jake asked.

I noticed Mavis and Ezzie were looking around the room and anywhere but at me or the men. I had no problem at all lying for my friends, but Jake was going to send someone up to dust for prints. And there was no doubt we would all be busted anyway.

"I wanted to carry a bag of rice up the steps to see if I could do it, so. . ."

"A bag of rice?" Jake interrupted me.

"Well we, or um I, asked Alexa, how much a human skeleton weighs. . ."

"A human skeleton weighs. . ." Alexa interrupted from the corner.

"Alexa, shut up," Hitch said, angrily.

"Hey, don't yell at Alexa, she exists to help you out." I said to Hitch, "There's no need to be rude."

"Sorry, I don't know that one," Alexa said, hearing her name again.

Hitch rubbed his forehead with both hands and stretched his eyes and face back in a gesture that clearly indicated his frustration, but was also a good way to get wrinkles I thought. I looked at Jake who had his eyebrows raised in a not-so-subtle invitation to finish my story.

"Anyway, '*you know who*' told me how much bones weigh,

so I went to the church kitchen to get twenty-five pounds of rice to see if I could carry it up the steps. I can, by the way, but it was exhausting."

"And you went alone?"

Dang, this guy was not easily distracted.

"Of course, she didn't go alone," Ezzie jumped in. "Don't be ridiculous. Why would anyone send their friend by themselves to a bell tower with twenty-five pounds of rice?"

Hitch rested his head in his hands and shook it. Hitch was overly theatrical sometimes if you ask me.

Fyndham left with his phone to his ear checking to see if the door had been processed. Hitch and Mavis went back to church with only one warning about staying out of things, and Ezzie and I went upstairs to figure out what I should wear on my date with Chad.

We decided Pazaluna was fancy enough for vintage Valentino. This was one of my favorite dresses, and I hoped Chad Everest was worth it. It was a caramel brown tank dress with a V-neck and cut low in the back. It had narrow vertical stripes made of copper and chocolate glass beading. The hem was swishy and had intricate green, rust, and caramel beadwork which formed a gorgeous, six-inch, floral border. It had kind of a twenties vibe and was a steal for seven thousand dollars.

"Is he tall enough for the copper Louboutin's?" Ezzie asked. Ez was five nine and thought about those kinds of things for other people but never herself. She would choose her Louboutins over a guy every time.

"I think so," I said, thinking I should have paid attention to something besides the dimples.

I had a beautiful pair of copper patent leather Louboutin pumps that were so shiny you could use the reflection to peer around corners. They had a four-inch heel which bumped me up over five foot nine, and I was pretty sure Chad Everest was taller than that. Oh well, not my problem if he wasn't.

She helped me do a twisted updo with a bun that was secured right below and behind my right ear. *I seriously hoped we weren't taking his stupid motorcycle*, I thought. *A helmet would kill this hairdo.* The whole look was flapper reminiscent.

Ez handed me a copper and brown beaded Chanel clutch that matched the dress perfectly. It cost more than double what the dress had, and I didn't even want to think that number out loud in my head.

"I love this purse. You can pull off brown perfectly with your gorgeous espresso hair," Ezzie complimented. Ezzie was the kind of friend who refused to let people call my hair brown; she always had an exotic name for it. She had perfectly highlighted blonde hair that hung just beneath her shoulder blades and not one of those perfectly highlighted strands would dare to be out of place. With her ridiculously deep blue eyes she was always a long cool bit of perfection.

"Hey, speaking of purses, the moms' group today had some seriously good knockoff Birkin bags, a Valextra, a couple of Tom Fords, a Gucci, and a Burberry."

"Huh, I wonder if they know they're knockoffs?" Ez asked, without doubting for one second that I would know them from an original.

"I don't know. It was weird to see them lined up at every-one's feet in a circle,"

"We can ask Mavis about it tomorrow I guess. I'm leaving my car here, Jake's going to pick me up when he's done with work."

"Ez, we are going to have to have a long Jake review tomor-row," I said. She just gave me an ear-to-ear grin and looked happier than I think I had ever seen her.

CHAPTER 4

Friday

"How was the date?" Ezzie asked, sauntering into the kitchen. Mavis, Hitch and I were sitting at the marble island eating scrambled eggs, bacon and a cantaloupe boat filled with fruit, yogurt, and granola. Ty had finished breakfast and was up in his room.

"Maybe I should be asking that question since I expected you last night and here you are at nine a.m.," I countered. I really didn't want to talk about my date in front of Hitch. Hitch made my knees wobbly and my breath shaky sometimes when he wasn't irritating the crap out of me. But he was my boss, and I desperately needed to keep things separate because I was virtually homeless and needed this gig.

"It was great. We stayed home and watched baseball and had pizza and beer."

You could have heard a pin drop as Hitch, Mavis, and I all stared at her. They had known her for only a month and even they knew that Esmeralda Bella Gold was not a beer and baseball kind of girl.

"Okay, we are definitely going to talk later," I said.

"So how was it?" Ezzie pushed.

"It was beautiful and delicious," I said.

"Oh no," Ezzie said. "I'm sorry."

"What are you sorry about? I just said it was beautiful and delicious."

"Yeah, I asked about your date and you described the restaurant," she said.

I hated how well Ezzie knew me sometimes. "Maybe I was

describing Chad," I said, getting a raised eyebrow from Hitch.

"Were you?" Hitch asked.

"No," I fessed up. "The whole night was too romantic."

"What is too romantic?" Mavis asked, "Is that even possible?"

"Yes!" Ezzie and I said at the same time.

"He came on his bike, so we took my car. He wanted to drive but nobody in their right mind hands over a million dollar car to a virtual stranger," I started.

"Most people in their right mind don't go out with a virtual stranger," Hitch interrupted.

"Sure, they do," Mavis said, "There's a whole internet industry that promotes nothing but stranger dating."

"Anyway," I continued, "when we got there, there were rose petals on the floor by the hostess stand. . ."

"Oh no," Ez said, getting there ahead of me.

"Yeah, they led back to a private banquet room, a whole huge room behind a curtain. I kind of wanted to sit out by the people and catch the vibe of the restaurant you know? Then there was a violin player who serenaded us while we ate."

"Did you get your own plate of food or have one long pasta noodle that you ate from opposite ends?" Hitch asked.

"Haha wise ass," I said. "The dinner was delicious, but then he had ordered champagne and chocolate-covered strawberries for dessert."

"Oh boy," Ez said, still shaking her head.

"Well, that sounds lovely," Mavis said without much conviction.

"This was a first date, sitting in the back room alone where there were zero distractions, just long meaningful glances that had no meaning. The worst part was on the ride to the restaurant he asked if I wanted to go to a wedding with him on Saturday. He said there'd be great food, a good band, and an open bar. At that point, he still seemed normal so I agreed."

"He was probably just nervous and went a little overboard," Hitch said. "Give the poor guy a chance."

"Yeah," I said glumly.

"You know Rabbi, you are very kind," Ezzie said to Hitch.

Hitch laughed at Ezzie and headed out. Mavis, Ezzie and I headed into the parlor and shut the pocket door behind us. Mavis pulled out a picture of Henry Olson, the one that they had recently buried, and put it on the board.

"Okay, I'm going to write the names of the MoGOs under the picture, and you can tell me what you think of each one," Mavis said.

"In general, they all seem smart, capable, confident, and mostly pleasant," I started. Then Mavis started pointing to the picture naming each member, as I gave a rundown on my impressions.

- *Kit Carlson - Short, blonde, cute, spunky, adventurous, and funny*

- *Laurel Lombardo - Classy, Type A, accomplished, perfectionist but not in an off-putting way, travel writer, black shiny hair*

- *Kendra Malcomb - Tall, striking brunette creative, out-*

spoken, witty

- *Lindsey Vanner - Blonde, skier, introspective, observant, smart*

- *Heather London - Actress in local theatre, adorable, shy but not a pushover, determined*

- *Kelli Reese - Sweet blonde, made the treats that day, seems a little like a better more healthy version of Martha Stewart*

- *Kelly O'Malley - Quiet but witty, smart, well-read, formerly a professor at Mankato State, dark hair*

- *Clair Clairmont - Smiley, looks like she'd be a ton of fun, confident, knows herself, good boundaries also an actress with Heather in local theatre*

- *Theresa Martin - Clair's good friend, grounded, fun and passionate, generous*

- *Mardi Heinrich - Capable, sweet, efficient, fun-loving, great laugh, seems like she could be a Velvet Hammer, auburn hair.*

- *Kristin Sells - Young, timid, sweet, unfortunate big nose, only single mom*

- *Leslie Ford - Wise, focused, cheerful, faith-filled*

- *Aubrey Sanderson - Classy, quiet, teaches Shakespeare at St. Timothy's, red-head*

- *Beth Johnson - Leader, long blonde hair severely pulled back, tall, rail-thin, slight southern accent, had been a former Southern Belle, reminded everyone she was really rich, judgmental, organized, no-nonsense, but philanthropic (as she reminded everyone twice, for those who much has been given, much is expected, blah, blah blah.)*

I looked at the board and cringed. "Mavis! Don't put anything about Kristin's nose up there."

"You said she has an unfortunate big nose."

"Well that was just a comment, it has nothing to do with anything. What's with you and Ez always putting big noses on the crime boards?" I asked.

"We're just thorough I guess," Mavis answered.

"Wow, how are we ever going to keep all of those people straight? Do we have to ask them all questions?" Ezzie asked.

"Well we don't have to focus on all of them, we'll just keep our eyes on them as a group and see if anyone sticks out. They circle up on Sunday mornings after church, so maybe you two could mention the bones then," Mavis said.

We all stared at the board for a bit. Nothing jumped out at us. I took a picture so I could peek at it later. Maybe some distance would help.

"Hello?" We heard a squeaky voice call from the kitchen. I carefully spun the board so our pictures faced the wall, and we headed into the kitchen, closing the parlor door behind us.

"Oh, hi there Lila," Mavis said, "Whatcha got there?"

"A Macaw, I think?" she said, "It was on the back porch."

There was a beautiful parrot in a cage. He, or she, had a red body and head with yellow, green, and blue wings. "Hello!" the bird said.

"Unbelievable," Mavis said.

"Someone dropped off a bird?" Ezzie asked.

"Cool!" Ty said, coming up behind us.

Mavis said, "everyone, this is Deacon Lila. I asked her to come over."

We introduced ourselves, and Mavis sent Ty off to research birds and figure out exactly what we had in our cage.

"So, what is a deacon anyway?" Ez asked.

"Well in the Lutheran church it's a called and ordained position."

"I need more words," I admitted, having no clue what she had just said.

"Being ordained is a ceremony the church has that declares that we are in a position to serve the congregation. Hitch is called to 'Word and Sacrament,' which means he serves inside a church. He preaches which is the Word part and does baptisms and can give communion. Deacons are called to Word and Service. This means we can preach if it makes sense to our position, but we focus on service. We have one foot in the world and one foot in the church. Grace in the Valley is unique because we are so service focused we have three deacons on staff. I work with the Community Center and am on the preaching rotation. Laura, another of our deacons, runs a food program and boys and girls club up in Hugo, but she is paid by our congregation. Jana, the third deacon, works with our youth and does respite preaching for smaller churches whose pastors need a sub so they can take a vacation or break."

"Wow," was all I could think to say.

"Mavis said you had some questions for me. Sorry I haven't been over sooner. I was on vacation during the whole Kramer and Anderson debacle, but have been meaning to come over and introduce myself."

"I'm Vivi, I'm so glad to meet you," I said. "This is Ezzie, she's my best friend and is here often. Ty and I were the ones who found the bag in the belfry. I know you were up there and was wondering if you saw anything?"

"Well I didn't see a bag full of human remains, that's for sure. I heard that the MoGOs were getting a tour and I had never been up there; plain old curiosity is why I went up. I went a couple of days before they did. It just looked like a belfry, nothing weird or unusual."

"Thanks," I said. "It's just kind of unsettling."

"It sure is," Lila agreed.

We chatted for a while and tried to get the bird to say more words without much luck. Lila and Mavis headed back to church; Ty, Ezzie, and I decided to go to Mangetti's for lunch.

*****

"Welcome," Mangetti greeted us at the door enthusiastically. "So, do you girls want a table or should I just show you right to my walk-in?" he laughed.

"A table will be just fine," I said, smiling at him. He was referring to the time Ezzie and I had been snooping in his restaurant because we thought he was killing rich guys and ended up getting locked in his walk-in cooler. Since we were there, we naturally helped ourselves to shrimp cocktails and gelato. And then there was that one other time I hid in there from the maniac who was actually killing rich guys.

Mangetti showed us to a table and said, "Chocolate and lavender martinis correct?"

Wow great memory, I thought. The waitress brought them over and took our order. Mangetti schmoozed a couple of tables and then came back and sat down with us.

"So, is this a social lunch, or are you tracking down another murderer?" Mangetti joked.

"Um, actually," I started.

"You're kidding me?" he said, looking at my face.

"We found a skeleton," Ty supplied.

"You're kidding me?" Mangetti repeated.

Ty and I took turns explaining about art camp and wanting to take a picture in the bell tower. Then we told him that the DNA proved it was someone who had been dead at least twenty years, but the name came up as a parishioner who was only buried about nine months ago. I pulled out my phone and zoomed in on the picture of Henry Olson that Mavis had hung on the board.

"This guy," Mangetti said, "His name's not Henry Olson, that's Jimmy the Butcher. No one can forget a nose like that."

"Please tell me he's the guy you buy your steaks from," I said.

"Nah, he used to work for Russo in Chicago. Jimmy took

care of some of his, uh, more sensitive operations in Chicago, Kansas City, and St. Paul. Everybody knew about Jimmy the Butcher."

"What do you mean everybody?" Ezzie asked.

"Those of us in the business world. We're all Italian, and when you're Italian you're family. Especially the restaurant business. It's a small world in the restaurant business, ya know what I'm saying?"

"So you, Russo, and Jimmy the ah, um, well Jimmy, were all in the family?" I asked.

"Well there's family, and then there's family. I mean I'm not a godfather to any of Russo's kids, but if it so happens he orders an extra truckload of steaks for one of his restaurants and would need help selling them, he would offer them to me rather than letting them spoil, if ya know what I mean."

I was pretty sure that in this scenario the truckload of steaks had very little "ordering" involved, and probably no steaks either. I was also sure I didn't want to know any more about it.

"Jimmy the Butcher's been missing for more than twenty years. He disappointed Russo back in the day and he disappeared. Rumor had it, Russo. . ." Mangetti paused, looking at Ty and then must have decided on a kinder, gentler version of the story he was about to tell. "Well, the talk was that Russo was kind enough to escort Jimmy and his old lady Shirley out of Chicago and invite them into a new living situation. A permanent situation, if. . ."

"Yes," I interrupted, "I know what you mean."

"But look at that, old Jimmy was hiding out right here the whole time. We were practically neighbors. You girls stay away from this, you don't want trouble with Russo."

Ezzie, Ty and I were finishing our lunches when Mangetti came back with gelato for everyone. "If you want to pop into the Speakeasy tonight, the password is 'Coconut Gelato.' That's in honor of you Miss Luxe. Give me a call anytime; I'll let you know the password du jour." Then he turned as the door opened, "Aw geez, these slime balls, excuse me, ladies," he said getting up from the table.

Since he had just told us stories about what I could only assume was a crime boss who everyone thought had murdered his unsavory employee without batting an eye, I was interested in seeing who he considered a slime ball. I spun around in my chair and was surprised to see Mr. Sheffield and the Macutty brothers. Richard Sheffield was my father's long-time money manager. I only knew Larry and Seph Macutty because my dad had despised them. I never paid much attention to what he said about business, but I knew he hated that Sheffield worked with them.

Mr. Sheffield's eyebrows shot up when he saw me, and he gave me the slightest of head nods. He was the one who had to break the news that Daddy had left the country to parts unknown and taken what money we had left with him. He had also helped me clear out as much stuff as I could fit into two moving trucks, handed me two thousand dollars in cash and a burner phone, and told me to lie low until Daddy could prove his innocence. Initially, I had thought that would be days and burned through the first thousand dollars in an instant, until he explained it would possibly be months, but most likely years, before my father could clear his name and that was only going to be possible if we found out who had set him up. Daddy had sent me a small gift and note a few weeks ago, so I knew he was safe, that he was hanging in there, and that he was thinking about me. I could tell Mr. Sheffield didn't want to draw Larry and Seph Macutty's attention to me and quickly walked past me.

"Vivi, do you know that guy?" Ty asked.

"Nope," I said, thinking, *dang this kid doesn't miss a beat.* My answer got an eyebrow raise from Ezzie since she had known Mr. Sheffield as long as I had.

*****

When we got home I told Ezzie, "I think we should put Larry and Seph Macutty on the board."

"You think they left bones in the belfry?" she asked.

"No, on the other side."

Besides the questionable deaths du' jour at Grace in the Valley, Ezzie and I had decided to try and figure out who had set up Daddy. In the past, we had used one side of the "crime board" for the Kramer-Anderson murders and the other side for the Daddy mystery. All we had on it was a picture of Daddy, another of Nick Mangetti, and a picture of "Il Posto di Vivi," the restaurant Daddy and Mangetti had owned together for six years.

Ezzie immediately grabbed a piece of paper out of the printer and drew two stick figures with ugly faces on them and wrote "Macutty Bros" under the pictures. That was one thing I loved about Ez. She was willing to go down a rabbit hole with me whether or not I was being reasonable.

We discovered there would be a celebration at dinner because Keith had found a job. It was at a small tech firm on the other side of the Twin Cities, but the pay was good and within a month or two the family would be able to move into their own place.

"We were living paycheck to paycheck," Kelli said. "When that company closed we lost the house we were renting. We're stoked that this job pays better and comes with benefits; we haven't had health insurance in six years."

Wow, by my count that was three babies without insurance. How was that possible? I wondered.

"The only bummer is, it's an hour commute each way," Keith said, as he got up and brought his dish into the kitchen.

"Thank God," Kelli said after he left the room. "With all this downtime he's been talking about having another kid."

"Yeah, probably a good idea to avoid that," I said, "there can't be many "K" names left."

"Ha, good point," Kelli laughed. "I worked as a CNA for a while but the daycare was way more than I would ever bring in. If we get our own place I might do daycare in our home at a reduced rate so other moms can afford to work."

"Wow, that's generous," Ezzie said. "Being a CNA seems to be a popular profession."

"The schooling is short and there are tons of jobs," Ashlee answered.

The kids were being silly and giggling. They were all trying to make Tootsie laugh by making faces and playing Peek-a-boo. Ashlee took her out of the high chair and started to clear her place. Tootsie was kind of cute, in that baby sort of way I had never paid attention to. I must have been staring at her because Ashlee said, "Do you want to hold her Vivi?"

Oh, heck no, absolutely not! was what I was thinking, but managed to say, "Oh you keep her, I'll grab your plate for you." Thinking a baby was cute and holding it were two very different things. Besides the volunteers, Shawna, and even Kelli, who I would have thought was babied-out, all grabbed her every time they could, so Ashlee got breaks.

Ez took off right after dinner. I passed on the strawberry-rhubarb pie. I had to start saying no to at least a few desserts a week if I wanted my clothes to fit, and I certainly couldn't afford to get new ones. Hitch popped his head in after everything was cleaned up and the volunteers had cleared out and asked if I wanted to take a ride.

He knew I had recently become a fan of riding on the back of his Harley. It was a gorgeous summer night, and I was thrilled to get onto the road with him. We had previously taken routes along the St. Croix River, but tonight we headed west towards St. Paul. It was fun riding through the mostly deserted streets of downtown. There were a few restaurants open but not much else.

"Do you want a malt?" he asked, rolling past a quaint dining-car diner that had been in a few movies shot in the Twin Cities.

"Sure," I agreed. Skipping dessert would have to wait for another day.

The diner was iconic, but I had never been inside before. We sat in one of the red leather booths. Hitch ordered chocolate and I ordered a mocha malt. They served them in old-fashioned fluted tulip glasses with the tin of extra malt on the side. It was fun to watch the traffic go by.

Hitch waved the waitress over and ordered a burger with a double order of fries for himself after asking if I wanted anything.

"Do you always get a malt first, then your burger?" I asked.

"I was going to just have the malt, but it made me hungry," he admitted, laughing. "I found out a little more about Henry Olson,"

"Which one?" I asked.

"The original, erh, bag of bones one," he said. "He and his wife were from St. Paul. They went to Washington High School and lived in the area their whole life. They took one vacation when they were seventy to Chicago and died in a car accident there. Some *high-rollers* paid for their funeral and to have them shipped back to Minnesota. No record of burial was ever found. But recently there was vandalism at a mausoleum at St. Timothy's Cemetery. All of the remains that were supposed to be in there were accounted for but there were two extra and curiously empty caskets found inside."

"Huh," was all I could think to say.

"Huh? That's all you have to say? That seems a little suspicious for a girl who has her nose in everything she shouldn't at Grace in the Valley."

"How is 'huh' suspicious? It's barely a word."

Hitch just sat and looked at me for a minute, and finally said, "Spill."

"I don't know anything," I said, trying to look as innocent as I could. I knew he would hate that we had gone to *Mangetti's*, especially since I had recently almost been killed there. But he just looked at me with that irritating expression that somehow made me want to confess to things I hadn't even done.

"You know how you're supposed to get back on a horse right away if you fall off," I started.

"Ah, geez," he said, with no provocation as far as I was concerned.

"Well, Ezzie and I went to lunch at *Mangetti's* today." I ignored the look on his face. "Nick sat down with us and was very apologetic about the whole, um, attempted murder situation, and well, one thing led to another and we mentioned we had uncovered a bag of bones."

"Oh good. I was afraid it wouldn't get out and was worried we would need to pay for advertising this week," Hitch said.

"Churches pay for advertising?" I asked, truly surprised.

"Yes, haven't you ever noticed the church page in the paper?" Hitch asked. I couldn't tell if he was serious or not. "Continue please."

"Well like I said, we mentioned that I had stumbled upon some bones and that it was baffling because they belonged to a guy who had been dead for twenty years but his name and ID matched a guy who had only been buried nine months ago. We showed him a picture of. . ."

"You happened to have a picture of Henry Olson with you?" Hitch asked, incredulously.

"Well, just on my phone, not an actual picture," I said, not liking how he was shaking his head. "Anyway, Mangetti took one look at it and said, 'That's Jimmy the Butcher!' and then we had gelato."

The gelato statement hadn't lightened Hitch's scowl like I had hoped it would. "Jimmy the Butcher?" he finally said. "How did he know that was who the fake Henry was?"

"Everyone knows Jimmy the Butcher," I said, channeling Mangetti and his *"what are ya, dumb?* tone of voice.

The waitress arrived with Hitch's food. He took half his fries out of the plastic basket in which they were served and put them on the plate with his burger and pushed the basket towards me. I would have never ordered them myself, but few things on this earth were better than piping hot french fries with a malt.

I explained that it was an interesting coincidence that Henry and Sharon had visited Chicago and died there and Jimmy and his wife, whatever her real name is, had also lived in Chicago. Then I told him how everyone thought Russo had 're-assigned' Jimmy, and Mangetti was amazed he was still alive and practically living up the road.

"Vivianna. . ." Hitch started.

"Yeah, yeah," I said. "Stay away from Mangetti." This was becoming a tiresome mantra.

Hitch pulled out his phone and called Fyndham. After repeating everything I had just said we finished and headed out. As we were getting on the bike I said, "now that this is a bigger case will Fyndham have to stop seeing Ezzie?"

"He will if he has an ounce of self-preservation," Hitch mumbled.

We headed to Shepherd Road and wound our way to the bluffs overlooking St. Paul and the Mississippi. Hitch parked the bike, and we walked a short distance on the path enjoying the view from our distant lofty perch. We were comfortably quiet, lost in our own thoughts.

"Vivi," Hitch said quietly, grabbing my hand to stop me, "I am not trying to be a spoilsport, but if Henry, or Jimmy, were connected in Chicago, this is nothing to mess around with."

I turned and looked up at him as he spoke. I could see the genuine concern in his eyes. Our proximity, the warm breeze, and his ridiculously handsome face drew me in. He brushed a strand of hair off my face and tucked it behind my ear, I rose on my tiptoes and moved my mouth close to his. He moved both of his hands to my shoulders and took a step back.

"Vivianna, I can't kiss you," he said. "As much as I might want to, I can't do it legally or morally."

What the hell? Was this a parole thing because he had been in prison? That didn't seem right, but admittedly I didn't know anything about how ex-cons were supposed to behave so who was I to say this was crazy.

"This is crazy," I blurted. "You did your time for, um, whatever it was you did, and now you should be able to have a normal, conjugal relationship with whomever you want, whenever you want."

Hitch threw his head back and started laughing which was rather irritating, then he pulled me in and held me to his chest. To say this whole encounter was confusing was an under-statement.

"This has nothing to do with my prison time," he said, "Clergy are legally prohibited from fraternizing in any way with parishioners or employees of their church. It's a church rule and a state law," he explained.

I thought about what he was saying for a few moments. "Well shit," I said.

"Indeed," he agreed.

"Do they know how much you pay me? Because I'm barely an employee at this rate."

"Yeah, the amount really isn't the point."

"Could you fire me for a few hours every couple of days and then rehire me?"

"That would probably be a lot of paperwork," Hitch said.

"I suppose," I conceded, feeling dejected. "This sucks. So, you can never get married?"

"Oh, I can be married, even to an employee. Each church has its own rules about that. I just can't date an employee," he laughed.

Since marriage was out of the question I took a step back and swallowed my disappointment. It was probably for the best. There was no good ending to making out with one's boss.

"Sorry I tried to kiss you," I said. "Can we just go back to you being irritated with me all the time and pretend that never happened?"

"I'm not irritated with you all the time," he smiled down at me, "but yes, let's take a step back."

Stupid principled pastor, putting a damper on a gorgeous night.

CHAPTER 5

Saturday

Saturday breakfasts were pretty casual because the families got up whenever they wanted. The breakfast squad had a yogurt bar set up with berries, chia seeds, walnuts, sunflower seeds, craisins, granola, and honey. There were bagels with a choice of schmeer and bacon.

Ezzie was already in the kitchen eating when I came downstairs. "When did you get here?" I asked.

"A few minutes ago. I was just about to come up."

We took our breakfast out to the backyard and ate in companionable silence for a few minutes. "I was with Jake when Hitch called last night," she said.

"Oh boy, how'd that go?" I asked.

"He wasn't thrilled that I hadn't told him about Mangetti. I told him I had forgotten all about it."

"Did he buy it?"

"I have a few tools of persuasion in my belt. I'm not sure he bought it but I convinced him to drop it," she grinned and I just shook my head. Poor Fyndham, he didn't stand a chance. "He had called in a request to exhume fake Henry a few days ago, it could even happen today. You would think he'd be thrilled because we jump-started the process for him."

"Yeah, go figure," I said, all sarcasm lost on Ez.

"So, what are you wearing tonight?" Ezzie asked

"I don't know, maybe the navy Halston?"

"Please tell me it's not a barn wedding. You can't wear Halston in a barn."

"No, it's in Stillwater at the Majesty, have you heard of it? It's supposed to be posh."

"How about the silver Huillier?"

"Oh, that might be perfect," I agreed.

****

I had a tea-length Monique L Huillier dress that was perfect. It was sleeveless and cut in a wide V in the back to the waistband. The front neckline was also a deep V to the waistband. It was daring, but the "V" narrowed significantly so there wasn't a lot of side boob to worry about. The underdress was silver silk and the overlay was sheer flowy gossamer with Swarovski crystals in a starburst pattern. It was sexy, twirly, and romantic. The perfect shoes would have been my silver moondust Jimmy Choo stilettos, but they were still in an evidence bag somewhere in the bowels of the Washington County Courthouse. I chose the ankle strap Via Sprigas with a four-inch heel. They had rhinestone-encrusted T-straps. My hair was in a curly, loosely twisted updo.

When I came downstairs to wait for Chad, Hitch and Mavis were at the house waiting for dinner. Hitch stared at the dress for a second, or five, longer than he probably intended. *Good*, I thought, makes up a little for the rejected kiss last night.

We parked at the Lowell Inn and took a limo-bus with some of the wedding party from there to Old Town Boat Works right on the St. Croix. It turned out the Majesty wasn't a venue but a four-level yacht. The ceremony and reception were going to be held there as it traveled up and down the river. The ceremony was on the beautiful top deck, the slow movement giving the space a perfect breeze for the balmy summer evening. Chad's sister looked radiant, and his family was friendly and welcoming. Really, really welcoming. Chad's mom introduced me to family members as 'Chad's Girlfriend,' which was awkward but I wasn't going to correct her since she was the mother of the bride and it was her big day too. Besides, I was pretty confident I would never see any of these people again so what did it matter. Right before we sat down to eat, Chad's grandma introduced me to her lifelong friend, Lydia, as 'Chad's fiancé' and the awkwardness rose to chin level. I was more than a little uncomfortable sitting at the head table with the family, but Chad was the brother of the bride so I guessed I shouldn't have been surprised.

The waiters had just cleared our plates when I heard a 'tink-tink-tink' next to me. Chad was tinking his fork on his water goblet getting everyone's attention, then stood to make a toast.

"Our family wants to welcome you all, and thank you for coming to celebrate Chelsie and Gary's new life together. Their love is an inspiration. In fact, if you are on the bride's side, keep this date open next summer because I anticipate we will be right back on this boat."

I clapped with the rest of the guests looking around for the cousin or friend who might be getting married. That's when I noticed Chad gazing at me with a dopey smile and his mom squealing with her hands on her cheeks like the kid from *Home Alone.*

Oh Hell No! was all I could think. I just gave a tight-lipped smile realizing it would be another three hours on this stupid tub before I could escape unless I wanted to dive off the side and swim to shore. I made an attempt to suck it up and pretend I was having fun.

The dancing began, and I did a circle dance with the bride and her friends, the *Electric Slide*, and a slow dance with Chad. Chad, for his part, was slamming *Mick Jagger's* and tried to talk me into one. Every, Single, Time he ordered. I explained, each and every time, that I didn't want Michelob and no, thank you, I didn't want a different beer, and no, dropping Jägermeister into the glass did NOT make it more appealing.

I could see the boat traffic getting heavier and knew we would be pulling into Old Town Boat Works soon. Chad was a little weavy, and it had very little to do with being on the water. Before I knew what was happening he left me on the dance floor and his sister Chelsie threw her bouquet to me. Not in the air, not over her shoulder, she called my name and flipped it to me. Unfortunately, instinct kicked in and I caught the stupid thing to everyone's cheers and congratulations. I slapped what I hoped was a polite smile on my face and ground my teeth together as we docked.

I was the first one aboard the limo bus and it was rolling on its first trip back to the Inn. We had to stop as Chad ran up and pounded on the door. "That was a close one," he chortled, as he sloshed his way onto the bus.

I could be a little nicer than I felt for a limited amount of time, but the 'affable meter' was coming critically close to combustion level. By the time we arrived at our destination, I had had enough. I pushed my way off the bus with Chad on my heels.

"Vivi, I'm in no shape to drunk, because I'm a little drive. But lucky for you, I figured that would happen and got us a room."

"Chad, all combined I have literally spent less than six hours with you. During that time you have acted like we were celebrating a five-year anniversary and basically convinced your family that we are getting married. What in the hell makes you think that any of this is even in the ballpark of being appropriate?"

"When you know, you know," he slurred.

"Well know this Chad. I am not marrying you. I am not

seeing you again. I am not answering your calls. Do not call me. Ever."

"Oh dear," I heard Chad's mother say behind me, "trouble in paradise?"

"There is no paradise, there has never been a paradise, and your son took three weeks to turn your check into church."

With that, I spun on my four-inch heels and walked away. I could hear footsteps behind me. I whirled around to see Chad dogging me, and raised a finger, pointing it in his face. "Don't!"

He seemed to get the hint, at least I didn't hear footsteps anymore. I could see people milling about down the street so I walked back towards the river and the action.

"Mavis," I said into my phone, "I need a rescue."

"Oh, for the love," she said on the other end of the line, "Where are ya then?"

"The Freight House in Stillwater, out on the patio."

"I'll be right there," she said as she hung up.

I ordered a tall gin and tonic and sat at the bar chatting with the bartender. The patio was full, I could see that on a different night it could be a fun spot. I would have to come back with Ezzie.

****

"You come here often?" I heard a low, familiar voice behind me.

"Is Mavis incapable of driving after dark or something?" I asked, as I turned and saw Hitch. It was the second time in not so many weeks that I had called her for a rescue from a bad date and both times she had sent Hitch.

He ignored my question and said instead, "You're a little overdressed for the Freight House."

"She's giving the joint a little class," the bartender said, "What can I get ya?"

"I'll just have charged water," Hitch said.

We sat and chatted and enjoyed the night air. I filled him in on the debacle that was my recent date and he only shook his head a little, which was polite. "Why is dating so hard?" I asked.

"Did you have better luck when you were rich?" Hitch asked.

"Sadly no, but I did have a credit card and could at least *Uber* myself out of whatever nonsense I had landed in."

"Well, you're going to have to get a card. I don't think it's safe to leave you alone on the mean streets of Minnesota without an escape plan."

"Ha," was all I could think to say but secretly agreed with him.

I left the bouquet with the bartender who immediately gave it to a waitress that he clearly had his eye on. "Just don't propose on the second date," I warned him.

We walked the half block to his bike, and I stood there while he put the helmet on my head, tightened the strap, and then patted the top. He never wore a helmet. I didn't see why I always had to, but we had already had this fight once, and I knew it was a waste of breath. I also didn't waste time trying to figure out the proper way of sitting on the back of a motorcycle with a skirt because that discussion had ended with the ever-helpful sentence, 'hike 'er up baby.' We took the long way home, and I told myself that Hitch probably enjoyed these late-night rescues because it gave him extra time on his bike. I refused to admit that I was pretty content leaning into his back enjoying an overwhelming sense of security, however false.

CHAPTER 6

Sunday

Church had just ended, and Ezzie and I headed over to the circle the MoGOs had formed in the lobby.

"Oh, hi Vivi," Kit Carlson said, when she saw me, taking a step back to open the circle for us.

"Hi everyone," I said, sweeping all the faces in greeting, "This is my friend Esmeralda."

"What a terribly interesting name," Beth said, almost sneering. "Is it ethnic?"

I was no more "woke" than the next WASP billionaire, but even I knew it was an odd question, especially directed at a person who looked like she belonged on a carton of *Swiss Miss*.

"It's a Spanish name that means emerald," Ezzie said. She maturely didn't wiggle her six-carat emerald in Beth's face to drive the point home. Ezzie's classy like that.

"You don't look Spanish," Beth continued.

"One of her parents' properties is a villa in Valencia, and they fell in love with the name when they stayed there," I jumped in.

Beth gave her a once-over from head to toe. You could see her sizing up the Carolina Herrera blue and white iconic bateau neck dress, matching blue Louboutin's, and her blue crocodile Birkin bag. My mind was clicking like a calculator, three thousand for the dress, seven hundred for the shoes, close to seventy thousand for the Birkin bag, I wondered if Beth knew her stuff that well. The slight dilation of her eyes when she saw the bag said she did. I had asked Ezzie to carry it to see if anyone noticed. Beth had a different Birkin bag than the one she had been carrying on Tuesday, equally fake, but still stunningly crafted. These were fantastically good knockoffs. And, like Thursday, all the other moms had their expensive fakes on their arms.

"So," Ezzie said, not giving Beth the time of day, "did you all hear there was a bag of skeleton bones found in the Belfry? I don't suppose you saw anything fishy when you were up there for your tour?"

"What on earth?" Kendra said, to a backdrop of gasps, 'no ways' and 'you're kiddings.' She immediately pulled out her phone and called someone.

Kit must have seen my raised eyebrow because she said, "She's probably calling her husband. He's some kind of big deal at the state attorney's office. She hates when he doesn't tell her stuff. And she used to be a news anchor, so she doubly hates to be left out. I hope she just leaves this alone."

"You think the state's attorney has already heard about this?" Kristin asked timidly.

"Don't be ridiculous, Kristin, it would still be at the local level," Beth said. "Besides, this isn't appropriate conversation for church," she added, glaring at the poor girl who took a step away from her.

"This is nice," I lied. "Do you all gather in the lobby every week after service?"

"Oh, my God, it's called a narthex," Beth said, sounding like I had personally insulted her dying mother.

"Good morning ladies," I heard Hitch say from right behind me. "Ezzie, Vivi," he added. I was going to assume he was singling us out because he knew us better, not because he thought we didn't qualify as ladies. We widened the circle to include him.

"Oh, good morning Reverend Hitchmayer," Beth effused, "wonderful sermon. I was just explaining to Vivi and Esmeralda that this was called a narthex, not a lobby."

"I'm sure they appreciated that," he said grinning. "Church words can be a little off-putting so it's nice to have a friendly tutor. You'll excuse me, I have some hands to shake." He gave a quick glance around the circle smiling. "I'll see you two for Sunday dinner, I assume?" he added, looking at Ez and me, and then broke away to talk to another group of people.

Beth's smile couldn't have disappeared off her face faster if it had used starting blocks. If I had to guess, I would say Hitch had said he would see Ezzie and me later just to rile up Mrs. Beth Johnson. *That wasn't very pastoral,* I laughed to myself.

Ezzie and I made our excuses and left the MoGOs in their huddle. We walked across the lot to the street, over to the shelter driveway, and up then up to the shelter. I was wearing wedge sandals and could have cut across the lawn to the house, but there was no way Ezzie was navigating the soft turf with her spiked heels.

"So, what did you think?" I asked.

"I think those are the best knockoffs I've ever seen. If you hadn't told me they were fakes I don't know that I would have noticed it."

"Not even the green one?" I asked.

"Well, okay, Hermes would never allow that snot green leather to come through their door."

"Agreed. It's why I took a closer look at the other bags. What did you think of the MoGOs?"

"That Beth is a piece of work," Ez said as entered the back door.

"Oh, hey Mavis," I said, seeing Mavis at the counter in the kitchen. She was dressed up so I knew she had been to church. "I didn't see you at church," I said.

"I went to the early service, then I had a few things to do at the office and came over here to hear how it went with the MoGOs."

"Why do they go to the ten-fifteen service? They're young, I thought at least some of them would prefer the contemporary service."

Grace in the Valley had six worship services every week. They held a mid-week service on Wednesday night with a focus on families and for people who worked weekends. There was a contemporary service on Saturdays at five in the afternoon, which was repeated on Sunday mornings at nine. It was a great service with a jazz-style band. They had some big names from around the Twin Cities and the music and vibe were relaxed but powerful. There was a "Sunrise" Service at seven a.m. on Sundays. The website said it was a time of prayer, communal chanting, and meditation incorporated with Taizé-style worship. I literally had no idea what half of that meant, but the lot was packed by six-forty-five every week, and it seemed to be mostly millennials going in. Then at ten fifteen they had their traditional worship. That service had several fantastic adult choirs, multiple children's choirs rotating through, and unbelievable organ music. They had traditional liturgy, which I had just learned was a kind of reading and response situation. I had never been in a church before but appreciated both the contemporary and traditional services. And Sunday evenings the youth team had a worship service run for and by high school and middle schoolers.

"Well I think that Beth loves it because she was Anglican or Eastern Orthodox or something," Mavis said. "Probably feels more familiar."

"And scares the rest of them into coming?" Ezzie suggested.

"Oh no, those women aren't pushovers. It's probably just

easier to get kids pulled together for the later service, then I think they go out to brunch afterward as a group with their families."

"How about Kristin? She seems scared to death of Beth," I said.

"Yeah, I didn't know churches had people like her; quite the attitude?" Ez said.

"Oh dear, was she abrupt with you two this morning?" Mavis asked.

"Nothing we couldn't handle, just seemed unnecessary," I said. "We've seen a million of her. She has no time for Kristin and me because she assumes we have no money, and she was threatened by Ez because it's clear she does. I've always been on the Ezzie side of getting snubbed before. This being poor thing is the gift that keeps on giving."

"So, you didn't care for Beth," Mavis said, leading us out of the kitchen and into the parlor. "Do we move her up on the crime board?"

"Nah, she's a straight-up bitch, but I don't think she would drag a bag of bones to the belfry. She'd be more likely to pay someone. Plus, she's a scrawny twig; I don't know that she'd make it." Ez stated.

"I'm not ready to cross her off," I said, totally aware it might have just been because I didn't like her and feeling okay about that decision.

"Anyone else?" Mavis asked.

"Kendra jumped on the phone the minute I asked about the bones," Ezzie said.

"Kit was full of information and said she wished she would leave it alone," I added. "I don't know if that meant she was worried about her or irritated by her digging into it more.

None of it screamed 'grave robber' however."

Mavis circled Beth, Kit, and Kendra. "Do you want to go meet Mrs. Jimmy the Butcher?" she said out of the blue.

Ez and I looked at each other, "Ah, yes please."

Mavis decided she would drive because her big old Ford Explorer wouldn't draw as much attention as my Cuda or Ezzie's Lamborghini. My car was a cool old muscle car, Ezzie's was ridiculous and barely street legal. She had a Lamborghini Aventador SVJ Roadster in a gorgeous 'blu aegir.' She had picked the color to match her eyes. It was one of the things we had in common. It was a nutty car to drive around the Twin Cities, but it was magnificent and turned heads which was the whole point of owning a fancy car.

We rolled down Rivertown Road past several big mansions that had been built by lumber barons when Stillwater was in its infancy, Mavis explained.

"Shit, that's Jake's car," Ezzie said, and then laid flat in the back seat. Fyndham wasn't in the car so I thought that might have been a bit of an overreaction.

"Well, Nelson's is down the road, let's go get ice cream and wait for *Detective Smokin Hot* to finish up," Mavis said.

"He is rather dishy, isn't he?" Ezzie agreed.

We sat in the Explorer and ate our giant cones. Mavis had rocky-road, Ez had rainbow sherbet, and I had rum cherry. Nelson's had great ice cream and even the single scoop was enormous. We drove the two blocks down to the river and explored a little of old Stillwater and then headed back to the fake Mrs. Olson's house.

"Grab the pie and the lily," Mavis said.

Grace in the Valley had a lovely tradition of giving loved ones a peace lily after someone died. We had recently used that and lemon pie to wheedle our way into someone else's house when we were looking for answers. Today it was French silk.

"Hello Sharon," Mavis said when the door opened.

"Oh, hello Mavis," the slender woman responded. Mrs. Jimmy the Butcher was about my height, which was right around five foot five. She had jet black hair, brown eyes that were so dark they looked black and huge boobs that sat so high and far apart you could have dropped a third one in the middle. Obviously enhanced. She was in her sixties I would guess, overly tanned and overly made up. She had fake eyelashes that were so long they'd make Tammy Faye Bakker weep. Again.

"This is Vivianna and Esmeralda, they're helping me on the grief team. We have a peace lily and some French silk pie. I brought paper plates and forks so all you have to do is pop some coffee on," Mavis said, stepping through the door. Dang, she was good. "Gee this must be a hard time for you. I'm sorry you'll have to go through the ordeal of bringing Henry, or um, you know, your husband, back up."

"Well you might as well know, my real name is Shirley Conti, not Sharon Olson. So, call me Shirley. Jimmy and I was in witness protection," she said, leading the way to the kitchen.

This might not be so hard, I thought, *she's kind of a yacker.* "So how long were the two of you in hiding?" I asked. "That must have been terrifying."

"We been outta Chicago for twenty years. Nick Russo put a hit out on us, and we got some help to make it look like we was in an accident, and then we disappeared. It all went pretty smooth actually," she said, looking like she was talking about something that had been no more bother than picking up a few items at the grocery store. "Oh, and a course the feds helped," she said as an afterthought.

"This is a beautiful home," Ezzie said, "Witness protection

must be more lucrative than I thought."

"Jimmy was in sales and did real good, especially these last couple a years," Shirley said.

I thought about Mangetti talking about Russo and how sometimes he had an extra truckload of "steaks." I wondered if Jimmy found himself with extra truckloads of things to sell as well.

"May I use your restroom?" I asked.

"Sure, there's a powder room across from the staircase," Shirley said.

Dang, I had desperately wanted to get upstairs, it seemed like that would be where all the crime-solving answers would be. I noticed there were five huge suitcases and a carry-on bag, all fake Burberry. Burberry didn't make the huge suitcases that were lined up but the barrel bag looked like it was authentic.

"Mrs., um. . ." I started, when I came back into the kitchen.

"Conti," she said.

"Oh, sure, well, Mrs. Conti, are you going somewhere? I couldn't help but notice your luggage by the staircase."

"I'm gonna visit a friend in Boca," she answered.

"Wow, steamy time of year in Florida," I said.

"Yeah, she ain't doin so hot, so I thought I would visit."

"Didn't detective Fyndham say you should stay in town?" Ezzie asked.

"Nah, he didn't mention that at all. Look, thanks a lot for the plant. Susan, my girl, will take real good care of it while I'm gone. But I'm gonna have to ask you ladies to leave now." With that, she stood up, and even Mavis was out of tricks to get us to stay any longer.

When we got outside we noticed a woman standing alongside a rather beat-up minivan in the driveway. She was pulling bags of groceries out of the back.

"Oh, hey there," Mavis twittered, "Can we give ya hand?" Mavis, Ez, and I walked over to the van and the woman looked confused. "We're from Grace in the Valley," Mavis said. "Mrs. Olson's church. We just stopped by to drop off a plant and some pie because we heard Mr. Olson was being exhumed and thought it would be hard on her"

"Oh, hello, I'm Susan Sells, Mrs. Olson's personal assistant," she said, tripping just a bit over the 'Olson'. "I wish that poor man could just rest in peace. Maybe they'll discover something that will give us some closure." Her eyes filled up with tears, but she got herself under control quickly.

"Oh, we thought he died of heart failure," Mavis said.

"Something was hinky about his death, that's all I'm saying," Susan said, a tear slipping from her eye.

"Have you worked for Mrs. Conti long?" I asked.

"Twenty-two years," she said, shaking her head like she couldn't believe it had been that long, then looked up with something between shock and fear at my use of Conti instead of Olson.

"So, you were with them in Chicago?" I pressed.

Since it was obvious we knew the truth about who the Conti's were and where they came from, she let her shoulders sag a bit and said, "Yes, Jimmy hired me as his secretary, but when they moved here Shirley ended up needing me more than he did. I had nowhere else to go and no marketable skills so I stayed."

I feel ya, sister, was all I could think. We helped bring the groceries to the back steps and headed out to the street to hop into the Explorer.

"Well, that was informative," Mavis said.

"Yeah," I agreed. "Susan's reaction was enlightening especially. Ez, what did you make of Shirley and Susan?"

"Mmm, hmm, what?" Ezzie asked. She was busy texting and had clearly not been listening to us. I just looked at her and waited for her to engage.

"Sorry, I was texting Jake. I think he should know Shiley has enough bags packed to leave for a month. Now, what did you say?" Ez asked.

"I asked what you thought of Shirley and Susan," I repeated.

"I think Susan was in love with Jimmy and hates Shirley," she said.

"I agree."

"Now how did you two come up with that?" Mavis asked.

"She misted up every time one of us talked about Jimmy. I don't care how good your boss is, after nine months that seems like a pretty strong reaction."

"Hey Mavis, are you going to be around tonight? I want to go check on my storage units and maybe rearrange a few things. Is it okay if I bring a few personal items to the shelter?" I asked.

"Oh sure, I'll come over after youth worship and have supper. I kind of like being there at night because I don't have cable at home, it lets me catch up on my old westerns."

*****

Ez and I changed out of our church clothes and into golf dresses. We grabbed the sandwiches left for us by the Food Squad and took them out into the sun to eat. The shelter had great summer furniture. There were two hanging porch swings on the front porch, and one each on the side, back, and upstairs porch. They also had a variety of rockers and wicker sofas. There was a fire pit area surrounded by brick pavers with a dozen sherbet-colored Adirondack chairs circling it. But best of all were the chair hammocks, regular hammocks, and lounge chairs with deep comfy cushions. I told Ezzie about my Friday night motor-cycle ride, the wedding and the rescue. She agreed that it was too bad, but probably a good thing that Hitch was off limits.

"He might be the hottest guy I've ever met," Ezzie said. "Most guys who try to do the bad boy thing just end up looking like 'try-hards' or they're actual thugs. But this guy is the real deal. I actually don't know how he does it. At any given time, he's the scariest and nicest guy in the room and both personas are genuine."

I knew what she meant. At six foot three, that alone was enough to make him imposing. But it was more than the rock-solid chest, big biceps, and overall size. He was always alert and aware of his surroundings in a way that made you feel like he saw everything in the room and in your soul. His near-black hair and eyes added to the intimidating vibe, but he was also loving and approachable, especially with the kids at the shelter and his parishioners. He was completely comfortable with who he was in any setting. And so insanely, distractingly handsome.

*****

It was just about dusk when Ezzie and I pulled up to my storage containers. Mavis let us take the Explorer in case I wanted to bring something back with me. Ez and I moved a few things around, grabbed the rest of my summer clothes, a Tiffany lamp, a pair of jeweled, French art deco candlesticks, and my summer eiderdown duvet and pillow.

"I really want to hang the 'Neiman' in my room," I said, looking at it longingly. My dad had commissioned Leroy Neiman to do a painting of the two of us riding. I was about seven, and we were galloping side by side on our property. Neiman's genius was capturing action, and you could see the tails and manes flying on both Arabella, my mare, and Dirk, dad's stallion. Dad only owned Belgian Blacks. He liked the Friesians because they were powerful but still had a ballet-like quality about them. I was a tiny thing with my hair flying as untamed as the horse's manes. I loved the intensity of the bright color and Neiman's ability to draw you into the moment even though the technique was impressionistic.

"I don't think it will fit in Mavis' car," Ezzie said, "and we are going to the Overpass."

"Good point," I agreed.

We covered the lamp and candlesticks with the duvet and headed over to the Overpass for a drink and a burger. The Overpass was where I had met Hitch the month before. I had called Ezzie to meet me there hoping she would help me figure out my next move. Hitch had overheard me and Ezzie ordering appletinis and smoke-infused bourbon and ran interference by ordering a vodka-seven with extra limes and a Beam on the rocks. Evidently he spoke dive-bar and we didn't. Then he heard me tell her I was sleeping in my storage unit, not my finest hour, and offered me the job at the shelter. Mr. Sheffield had told me to steer clear of any place where I might run into people I knew, and this was the seediest place I had ever seen outside of a TV set. There was a literal zero percent chance that anyone from my former life would see me here. This was the neighborhood where Hitch had grown up, and everyone in the bar had treated him with respect and something akin to awe. Oddly it was the exact reaction he got from his parishioners.

"Hi Sarge," I said, greeting the bartender when we walked in.

"Hey Appletini, how're doin? I would have bet money I'd never see you in here again," he said.

"I'm fine, thank you. How have you been since we last met?" I answered him. Apparently, that reply was hilarious, because he threw his head back and laughed. I looked at Ez and she just shrugged.

"I have something for you," I said, pulling out the Apple Schnapps.

"What the hell do I do with this?" he asked, shaking his head.

"Just mix it with vodka, shake it on some ice and pour it into a martini glass."

"Well on your next visit, you'll have to bring a shaker and martini glasses," he laughed.

"I'll just have mine on the rocks in any old glass," Ez said.

"Regular-sized ice okay with you?" Sarge asked, smirking at her.

The last time we were in Ezzie had asked for two-inch cubed ice. It was a pretty standard request at the bars we had frequented in my former life.

"I'll suffer with whatever you have," she smiled, "and I'll have the shrimp po-boy basket."

"I'll have the same," I added, looking up at the menu on the chalkboard above the kitchen serving window, "but make mine a pulled pork basket," I added to Sarge's retreating back.

"Bold choice with the white dress," Ez said.

We had both changed before we came over. We wanted to

keep things casual. I had on a Kate Spade, white eyelet sundress, and Ezzie had a black Halston cross neck halter jersey-knit dress. I had on simple Jimmy Choo white patent cork wedges with an ankle strap and Ezzie had on black Tori Burch flat sandals making us about the same height.

Sarge dropped off our drinks then went off to order or possibly make our food. I spun around on my barstool to get a better look around the room. I couldn't be sure but it seemed to me that the room was full of the same exact people, in the same exact places, wearing the same exact clothes as the last time I was here. Ezzie and I had a second drink, and I had just successfully swallowed my last bite of pulled pork without incident when the two men who had been playing pool came up on either side of us.

"So, you two mamas looking for a good time?" the one with the leather vest standing next to Ezzie said. I couldn't take my eyes off his tattoo. It was a snake that wrapped around his neck twice and ended by his right ear with its jaw wide open like it was going to bite off the lobe.

"Mamas? Really?" Ez said.

"Yeah," the guy next to me said. "I call you mama and by the end of the night you'll be calling me daddy." He was considerably shorter than the guy with the ear in jeopardy but was meaty and looked like he had been in too many fights.

"Mmm, yeah, that's not going to happen," I said.

"Well, you don't show up dressed like that without hoping for some action," the guy next to Ez said.

"I'd leave it alone boys," Sarge said, strolling over towards us from the other end of the bar. As he finished his sentence the door opened and I could feel the warm summer breeze and humidity waft over my back.

"Yeah, why's that?" Mr. Meaty asked.

BONES IN THE BELFRY

"That's why," Sarge said, nodding towards the door.

The two guys turned around but before Ezzie or I could spin in our chairs I heard Hitch's voice saying, "Snake, Ralphie, you're both lookin' good, can I buy you two a beer?"

He pushed his way between me and the man who had to be Ralphie, wrapped his hand around the back of my neck, and tilted my head back as he leaned in and gave me a knee-weakening, breath-stopping, heart-pounding kiss. A kiss that went on a few seconds longer than was respectable for a public greeting. Or for a pastor.

"Hey Hitch," Ralphie said, stepping back. "No hard feelings man, didn't know this lady was claimed."

Claimed? There was so much wrong with the last two minutes I didn't even know what to sputter first. Hitch did a circle thing with his finger and Sarge grabbed three bottles of beer from the cooler and handed one to Snake, one to Ralphie, and one to Hitch. Since Hitch had clearly marked his territory, Ralphie moved to stand by Snake.

Ezzie looked at me and said, "Well at least he didn't pee on you."

I was trying to decide if I was furious with, or grateful to, the Reverend Hitchmayer when Snake said, "Daisy sounds good."

"You've always had a great ear," Hitch said.

"Daisy?" I asked.

"Hitch's bike," Snake said, without a smirk or a snicker. I couldn't tell if it was because he was afraid of Hitch or he saw no irony in a Harley named Daisy.

"Your bike's name is Daisy?" I said incredulously.

"Yep, you can't tell me you haven't named your car?"

"Well yes, but I didn't know guys named their bikes."

"We do. Let me guess, you named your car Khloe," Hitch said.

"Is that a Kardashian reference?" I asked, as he just smirked and took a swig of beer. "Her name is Wanda."

"Nice, *A Fish Called Wanda*, I get it," Hitch said, nodding in approval.

"What does she drive?" Snake asked Hitch.

"*She* drives a '71 Cuda convertible," I said, emphasizing the 'she'.

"You're kidding,"

"No way," Snake and Ralphie said at the same time.

"Couldn't be more serious," Hitch said. "And that one drives a Lamborghini Aventador SVJ Roadster," he said, nodding towards Ez.

"Named Sophia," Ezzie added.

"Sure, ya gotta, they're both hot Italians," Snake said, nodding his approval. He turned to Hitch and said, "Let me know when you're ready to throw a *'Jekyll and Hyde'* on 'er" and stepped away from the bar. "Thanks for the beer."

"Yeah thanks, man," Ralphie repeated.

When they were back at the pool table Hitch looked at us and said, "Have you two lost your minds? What would you have done if Sarge hadn't called me?"

"You're mad at us?" I said, feeling a slow burn rising from my belly. "You are seriously mad at us? We were fine and then you waltz in acting like the First-base Friar and . . ."

". . .saved your ass," he interrupts. "What are you even doing here?"

"I needed to grab some things out of my storage unit and thought I would bring Sarge the bottle of Sour Apple Schnapps I got for him."

"Stole for him."

"You stole booze for me?" Sarge asked. "Nice, that means a lot."

Hitch gave him a withering eye. "Do I even want to know what you got out of storage?"

"Not that it's any of your business," I said, "but I needed some more clothes."

"Ha," he snorted.

I ignored him and continued, "My summer quilt, a pillow, a lamp, and some candlesticks."

Hitch took a deep breath and slowly exhaled. "You do realize even that small amount of stuff could get stolen just sitting outside. I know it's not worth all that much but still."

I looked at Ez, who had sucked her bottom lip in and was studiously avoiding eye contact with Hitch while she looked for something non-existent in her purse.

"What?" Hitch said, looking between us.

"You know you and Fyndham have a lot in common," Ezzie said, valiantly trying to change the subject.

"How much money is sitting out in that Explorer?" Hitch asked.

"Oh, who keeps track of money," I answered, almost rolling my eyes at myself since I had recently become a walking calculator.

"Esmeralda?" Hitch said, looking at Ezzie. Great, I thought, he must think she's the weakest link. Ha, is he in for a surprise.

"Well the candlesticks are probably the most expensive things," she offered up without a thought. Then seeing my face, "what, the lamp is only around sixteen right? The candlesticks are worth way more."

Ezzie had been with me when I had the candlesticks wired so they could be used as bedside lamps. I figured I should have the Tiffany lamp rewired at the same time. It was from the early 1900s and still had cloth-covered wiring which didn't seem safe.

Hitch spun to look at me, "You have a sixteen hundred dollar lamp out there?"

"No!" I said. "Sarge, can we get our tab?" I added hoping to change the subject.

"Viv?" Hitch said,

"It's closer to nine," I admitted.

"Nine hundred dollars?" he said.

"Ummm, you know, thousand, but it's under the quilt with the candlesticks."

"Which are thirty thousand," Ezzie piped in.

"Ez!" I said, shocked she would play the traitor.

"Oh come on, I have stuff to do tonight, and Sir Ask-a-lot over here isn't going to back down. There's a nine thousand dollar eiderdown quilt, yes, they can run that high. A five thousand dollar eiderdown pillow and probably another hundred K of clothes. Can we go now?" Ezzie stood up, put her purse on her arm, and took a few steps towards the door.

"Are you shitting me?" Hitch said.

"Well, I don't think vulgar language is necessary, but no, she is not *shitting you*. I don't think you have a good grip on how much things cost in the normal world," I said, hopping off my barstool, giving Hitch a shove to get him out of my personal space as I did so.

Sarge laid down the bill and said, "Thanks ladies, come back any time. Seems like you've made some friends," and he walked away smiling.

I grabbed the bill and was shocked by how cheap everything was. Although I guess it should be since Ez and I had supplied the liquor.

I looked up at Hitch, "Um, can I borrow twenty bucks?"

"Unbelievable," he said, digging in his wallet.

CHAPTER 7

Monday

By the time I came down everyone was out of the house. The kids started a new week of Sports Camp. Elementary-aged kids were on campus doing something sporty, I hadn't really paid attention. Middle and high schoolers were touring the different sports facilities in the Twin Cities. Mrs. Schmidt had put up a stink about letting Ty ride the bus, but Hitch had put a pretty quick stop to her nonsense.

The Food Squad had left the coffee on, so I poured myself a cup and then padded over to the fridge in my bare feet to grab some fruit and yogurt. I tucked my feet under me and sat at the island. I was about three spoons into my yogurt when the back door opened and Hitch walked in. He didn't say anything; he just walked over to the coffee pot, poured himself a cup, and sat across from me at the island.

"Look, Vivi, about that kiss. . ."

"Stop!" I interrupted. "I get it, you thought you were rescuing us. Don't worry I won't start passing you notes in class, or stalk you on Facebook. Let's just drop it."

"For the record, I was rescuing you," Hitch said with a crease between his eyebrows, looking stern and exasperated.

I looked at him for a few seconds. He wasn't the only one exasperated. "Reverend Carson Hitchmayer, I know you think that I am shallow, oblivious and dimwitted. Frankly, it's getting a little old. Do you really think Snake and Ralphie are the first two guys who have hit on Ezzie and me?"

He looked at me for a bit without speaking, then finally said, "This is the second time you have accused me of thinking you were dumb. It didn't go down all that well the first time, so I will say it again, I do not think you are stupid. I never have. Just answer a question for me. Before your dad skipped town, what was the last bar you were in?"

I thought about it for a minute and said, "The Farrington at the top of the Q."

"Guys in three thousand dollar suits, staying in four hundred dollar a night rooms, right?"

"Well the VIP suite is fifty seven hundred, and the suits are closer to eighteen thousand, what's your point?"

"My point," Hitch growled, running his hand through his hair, "is this, Miss Luxe. I'm sure you and Ezzie get hit on in every bar you grace, but last night you were out of your league."

I looked at him for a minute and tried to get the anger that was beginning to boil under control. "How many of the people who were in the Overpass last night can you name?"

"I don't see what. . ."

"How many?" I snapped, thinking *two could play the 'ask questions' game.*

"All of them,"

"That's what I thought since that is where we first met you. I'm going to go out on a limb and assume that the bar you frequent is not a well-known hangout for rapists, serial killers, and kidnappers."

"No, but they aren't choirboys either, Vivi. These are rough men, and I am going to say it again, you were out of your league."

"Do you know what guys who wear twenty thousand-dollar suits and don't blink an eye at staying in six thousand dollar a night rooms don't hear very often?" I asked. Without waiting for an answer, I went on. "They don't hear the word 'no.' Much like the boys at the Overpass, I'm betting a percentage of them buy and use drugs. These guys also buy women, and they buy loyalty from sycophants. They live in a world where people bend over backward to kiss their empowered asses. They are entitled and absolutely believe it is their right to possess anything they want. They, too, are dangerous men. Men are men, Hitch. Some advertise their manhood in Armani, others with a snake tattoo, the main difference is location and fashion choices. Ezzie and I have navigated these waters since we were fifteen. We know we're not bullet-proof, but we're not careless, clueless or helpless either."

I put my spoon in the dishwasher, walked out of the kitchen, and went up to my room.

*****

Ez and Mavis came over for lunch, and we grabbed a sandwich and some chips since we were on our own. No families meant no Food Squad. We brought it all into the parlor and shut the door behind us. I wasn't in the mood for any surprise appearances from the most Reverend Hitchmayer.

"Well let's put up a picture of Shirly and Susan," Mavis said, pulling them out of her bag.

Under the pictures, I wrote 'Shirley Conti aka Sharon Olson - 60' and 'Susan Sells- 45' "What else should I put under there?"

"Oh, good guess on the ages, Mavis said. "I looked them up and Shirley is 62, Jimmy was 70 when he died. And Susan is 46."

I added the correct ages to those three then I looked over the other names on the board. "I'm going to call the MoGOs as a group thirty-ish," I said.

"Except for Kristin," Ezzie piped in. "She can't be much over twenty."

"She's twenty-one," Mavis said. "I know because I looked it up when she had the baby baptized; she seemed so young."

"Under Susan you should put 'had a thing for Jimmy.' I still say she was way too sad for a casual employee," Ezzie said.

"Well she has worked for them for twenty two years, but I agree, there was more there."

"So, we have a bag of bones that's right around twenty years old, an employee that has been around for twenty two years, the Conti's in witness protection for twenty years, and a young woman who is twenty one. That's a lot of twenties, think that means anything?" I said as I connected all the numbers with blue strings.

"Shirley also had fake Burberry luggage, but she had a real bag too," I added as an afterthought.

"More people have fake designer bags than real ones," Ezzie said.

"I know, but it's odd that I've seen so many in the last week," I insisted.

"Well put 'Knockoff Designer Bags' up there if they're bugging you. Do you think the Feds always give people in witness protection other people's IDs? That seems weird. I mean both Conti and Olson came up when the police started digging. They're the Feds for crying out loud, why not give them a new social security number?"

"I think we should add Russo too," Mavis said. "If he had a hit out on Jimmy, maybe he finally found him and killed him."

"Sure, but why bring a bag of bones to the church bell tower?" I asked.

"As a warning to Shirley that he knew who they were pretending to be?" Ezzie guessed.

"Oh, that's pretty good, Ez. Explains why Shirley wants to get out of town, too. I agree." I wrote 'Ru' on the board and stopped. "If he has been on the church campus, or more likely sent someone to do his dirty work, I don't think I feel safe having anyone accidentally, or purposefully poking their noses in here and seeing that we're on to him."

My fear must not have been too out of line because Mavis and Ez didn't scoff and they both looked thoughtful for a few seconds.

"Put Dean Martin," Mavis suggested. "He's a famous Italian and it can be code."

"Speaking of Italian's, should we add Mangetti? Again." I asked.

"He seemed genuinely surprised that our Mr. Olson was Jimmy the Butcher," Ez said. "But he did know who he was, and does business with Ru. . . err Dean. By the way, Jake confirmed that the door had adhesive residue but no usable prints," she added.

"Okay, well let's take Janitor Mark and Deacon Lila off the board then. I mean I never really suspected Deacon Lila and even though that janitor is scary as hell, he was up there before the MoGOs. Actually, we can eliminate anyone with a key because why would they need to tape the door open if they had a key?"

"Do you think it was someone in that mom's group?" Ez asked.

I looked up at the list. We had Beth, Kendra and Kit circled, none of them for very good reasons. It could be any of them.

"Hey, Kristin's last name is Sells. Is she related to Susan?" I asked Mavis.

"I don't know," Mavis said, already pulling up church info on her telephone. "The baby became a member when she had it baptized but she's not an official member. We don't have any extended family information listed."

"Do you usually?" Ezzie asked.

"Sometimes, "Mavis said. "If they have someone listed as an emergency contact, if they were a sponsor for the baby, or on the approved pick up list for kids for Sunday School or camp. Or if there is more than one generation or family member at the church then the data program will pull up family associations."

"How about that?" was all I could think to say.

"I have her address; want to go visit?" Mavis asked.

"Does she need a peace lily?" I asked.

"No, but it never hurts to bring pie," she said.

*****

Mavis, Ez and I, along with a banana cream pie, pulled into a trailer park that was only a few miles from the church.

"I don't get it," Ez said looking around. "Who would build a trailer park on the edge of a golf course? I mean I kind of get it in Arizona I guess for snowbirds but, golf course frontage is worth top dollar."

"I don't know," Mavis said, "maybe the trailer park was here first?"

We pulled into Kristin's driveway. It was a neat little mobile home. White exterior with black window trim and shutters. She had a few wooden steps leading up to her door with a small five by five foot deck. I had never even driven past a trailer park before; this was fascinating.

"Oh, hi Mavis and Vivi, and um, Elizabeth, right?" Kristin

said when she opened the door.

"It's Ezzie," I corrected her.

She immediately invited us in. I was a little disappointed because watching Mavis talk her way into a place was kind of a thing of beauty.

"We brought pie to share," Mavis said chipperly.

"Uhh, okay," Kristin said. "Do you want milk or lemonade with it? Sam and I don't drink coffee, so we don't have a pot."

"Water will be fine for me," I said and Ezzie and Mavis agreed. I was so happy we had brought something with us because the sparse and ragged furnishings made it pretty clear that Kristin didn't have much.

We went into the kitchen where there was a contraption with high sides and netting all around it and a baby sound-asleep at the bottom.

"Do you want us to wait in the other room?" I whispered.

"Oh no, we're fine," Kristin said in a normal volume. "We've kind of trained him to sleep through normal noise. It's not a quiet park, and I didn't want to tippy-toe around my own home."

"Huh, that's brilliant," I admitted.

After the pie was served and the remains were put in the fridge, Kristin asked "So what brings you all out to the trailer park?"

"Kristin, we met Susan Sells yesterday at the, um, Olson's house," I said, not sure if I should be saying Conti, "We were. . ."

"Wondering if she was my mom?" she interrupted. "She is. I also know their name is Conti. I grew up with the asses."

"So, you're clearly not as sad as your mom about Jimmy's

death," Ez said.

"My mom routinely worked twelve hours a day for them for peanuts. She kept their stupid secret all these years. They made a killing off those handbags. The rich just got richer and the poor got chewed up and spit out."

The door opened and a young man walked in and looked around the kitchen. He had dishwater blonde hair that fell in his eyes, and he swept it back with his right hand. He was a nice enough looking guy but had a sneer on his face that kind of made me want to slap him. I didn't know if he was angry that Kristin had company or if he always wore his face that way.

"Hey babe," Kristin said, "these are some friends from church. Vivi is the House Mother at the shelter and just joined the mom's group."

'Mr. Chuckles' turned to look at each of us and the sneer lightened into a scowl which was only slightly better. "Hi," he said begrudgingly. "House Mother?"

"It's more of an administrative role," I sighed.

"They brought banana cream pie," Kristin said.

"Really?" he said, his face brightening. Hmmm, maybe he was just hangry.

"Sam Keiner," he offered as an introduction, heading to the fridge and the pie. "I'm Jamie's dad."

"Well, Sweet Baby James sure is a good little napper," Mavis said, smiling at the baby contraption.

"They met mama yesterday," Kristin blurted.

I had been nervous to return to the Susan subject but since she brought it up I said, "Shirley had a bunch of luggage packed and ready to go when we stopped there yesterday. We found it odd that she would take off right as they were about to exhume her husband's body. One would think she would want to stay and find out if anything was amiss."

"Amiss? I'll tell you what was amiss, that bitch and the son of a bitch she was married to."

"Oh, let's not even talk about them," Kristin interrupted. "I'm just happy mama is moving on."

"Really?" Mavis said, sounding as surprised as we all felt.

"Yeah, she's renting a small house in St. Paul and got a job downtown as an assistant manager at Greenway Restaurant."

"Oh, good for her," I said, not really knowing if that was good for her or not.

When baby Jamie woke up, Kristin picked him up and started nursing. Sam's scowl melted into a dopey look that radiated such pure love I felt bad that I had such a harsh first impression. We said our goodbyes and hopped into the Explorer.

"Wow, those two sure dislike the Contis," Ezzie said.

"I wonder what she saw growing up that makes her hate them so much," I added.

Ezzie's phone rang and she nestled into the seat behind us and mumbled and cooed into the phone, so I figured it must be Fyndham. Mavis and I chatted and gave her some privacy. The vehicle had so much space it wasn't hard.

We were pulling into the church lot when Ezzie hung up. "Jimmy the Butcher was poisoned," she said.

"Fyndham is telling you details of the case?" I asked, surprised.

"There was a leak and reporters showed up. He's furious. I think telling me, so we know first, is his tiny bit of revenge."

"I wonder if Kristin or Sam hated Jimmy enough to poison

him," I asked. "It seems like a leap to go from hating someone to killing them."

"All I know is that when this comes out on the news I bet they're going to regret having talked to us so candidly," Ezzie said.

I hugged Ez goodbye. She was headed to Boston for the 4th. It was a long-standing date with Stephen. I couldn't wait to hear how the Fyndham conversation was going to go. She was determined to tell him about Jake and didn't seem one bit nervous. *Better her than me*, was all I could say.

CHAPTER 8

Tuesday

I woke up to shrieks and giddy laughter. Ty, Shayna, and the older Ks didn't have camp because it was the 4th. The little girls were already sporting their patriotic boas and there was an air of excited mayhem that carried all the way up to the third floor.

"Vivi," Ty said, running up to me, "How did you sleep so long?"

"It's eight o'clock on a holiday," I laughed. "That's hardly sleeping in."

"Pastor Hitch said the whole house could have a picnic by the pond. He said I could try and swim across if I could find someone to do it with me and find someone to row alongside us."

"Oh, he did, did he?" I said. "Did he have any suggestions?"

"Well, he thought Keith would be good in the boat because the whole idea is to have someone strong enough to pull us in if we got tired."

"Mmm hmm."

"And he thought maybe someone who had grown up on a lake might be a good swimmer."

"Mmm hmm," I said again.

"Vivi, can you do it with me?"

I didn't know who was pulling the strings on this outing, Ty or Hitch. Ty and I had recently tried kayaking, and I had told him I grew up on a lake. I couldn't remember if Hitch knew that or not. I didn't know if it was one or both of them conspiring, but either way, I had almost zero ability to say no to Ty.

"Sure," I agreed, "I'll have to take a better look at the pond from ground level though to see how far the swim will actually be."

"It's a little over two hundred yards," Ty said.

"Hmmm, you had that answer ready to go. Now how would you know that?"

"Pastor Hitch might have mentioned it," he said, staring at his shoes.

"Okay, I'll be back for lunch and we can give it a shot," I laughed. Dang that kid; I was a total sucker for his shenanigans.

I ate a cinnamon roll out on the back porch watching the kids fill up water balloons in preparation for the picnic this afternoon. When I was done I grabbed some coffee in a to-go mug and headed out the door. I wanted to go back to the Conti's to see if Shirley had slipped out of town. When I pulled up I could see Susan's van in the driveway but no sign of Shirley. I didn't know what that meant since we hadn't seen Shirley's car last time we were here either. I parked and went to the front door. Before I could even knock Shirley pulled the door open.

Shirley was in a wildly colored caftan. It was sheer and I could see the black bikini underwear and lack of bra she had on underneath. If I had had any doubts about the plastic surgery on the last visit, which I didn't, this would be proof beyond a reasonable doubt. My boobs hadn't been that high and tight in seventh grade. They really were a wonder of engineering. I speculated about the possibility of some sort of internal truss system.

"Hello Victoria," she said.

"It's Vivianna," I corrected.

"Oh," she said boredly. "Come on in. Would ya like a Mimosa or Bloody Mary?"

"No, thank you," I said, thinking, it's not even nine o'clock on a Tuesday. "Actually, I have a couple of questions if you don't mind."

"I don't mind, I suppose, but who are ya again, and why d'ya care?"

"I'm the one who found the, um, first Mister Olson's bones in the belfry," I said, stumbling over what to call everyone. "And I'm just nosy."

"Well I can respect that," she said, waving me to a chair in the breakfast room. "Where's your friends?"

"I'm not sure what Mavis is up to, and Ez is in Boston for the 4th. She'll be back Thursday or Friday depending on how a tough conversation with her fiancé goes."

"Ugh, I'm glad I'm too old to be dealin with them issues," Shirley said.

"So, Shirley, I am just so fascinated with this idea of having to give up your whole identity and pretend you're someone else. What was that like, and how did you even know about the Olsons?" I was hoping that she wouldn't notice that I assumed she knew the Olsons rather than it being the Feds who assigned them that identity.

"My ma grew up in St. Paul, down by the old 'Spaghetti Junction' before they tore it up. The Olsons was her neighbors. Two more boring human beings God has never put on this earth. Granted, I was just a kid, so all old people was pretty boring to me. I continued to send them Christmas cards and stay in touch after I moved to Chicago and married Jimmy. Partly outta habit I guess and partly outta obligation. They was my mom's caregivers in her last months. She died of liver failure. It wasn't a pretty way to go. Anyways they took a Golden Anniversary trip to Niagara, and on their way home they called from Indiana and said they was gonna swing by and say hello. It sounded like they was lookin for a place to stay, but Jimmy and I didn't have the kind of lifestyle that two old Minnesota birds would appreciate if ya knows what I mean. I warned them that Chicago drivin wasn't for the faint a heart and maybe they should just loop around the city, but they wouldn't listen.

"The next day the police comes to the door. Jimmy immediately panicked and says, 'I can get ya all the info on Russo that you want, I'm willin to make a deal.' Turns out they was just comin to tell us that the Olsons had been in a car accident and we was the only names and numbers they had on 'em. They didn't have any kids and had outlived the rest of their family. So, we went down to the morgue and claimed all their personal possessions which included their passports, bankbooks, and all the things ya should have locked up but old people carry with them. We paid cash to have their bodies sent back to Minnesota and put in a mausoleum at St. Timothy's. Jimmy knew a guy who worked there who owed 'im. He was able to slip them in with a family that he said would never know the difference.

"The next morning the Feds are knockin on the door and says they was interested in hearin about Russo. Jimmy told them he was kidding, that it was a funny bit he did whenever he runs into any cops. Everyone knows Chicago PD has more leaks than a straw roof, so we knew Russo would be hearin about what Jimmy had said, so we grabs the Olson's paperwork and just slipped into their life. We lived in their house for about five years until we could get established and here we are."

I had no idea what to say to all that. "Wow," I said, after a second or two.

"Yeah, 'WOW' seems to sum up my life," she said. "I wasn't thrilled to be home. I had left for the bright lights, ya know what I'm sayin, and here I was back in the same neighborhood I tried like hell to get outta. St. Paul had been part a Jimmy's 'retail area' for Russo, so we was both pretty comfortable at least. I just wanted to live a normal life, ya know, maybe have us a couple kids. But Jimmy, he always liked the high life. He got back into sales, and I think he was doing so good Russo mighta heard about it. Lookin back, I guess maybe the heart attack might notta been the way he died."

Hmmm, I guess Fyndham hadn't been by with the poison news yet. "Well, thank you so much for indulging my nosiness. I was worried for you with all this unfortunate upheaval."

"'Unfortunate upheaval' that's a good one," Shirley snorted.

I wasn't sure I believed her whole story, but parts rang true. I saw Susan loading boxes by the side door on my way out. Her mouth was set in a grim line, and she did not look very happy. I walked over and smiled and said, "Hi Susan, it seems every time I see you, you're hauling something."

"Yes, that's the glamorous life of working for the Contis. No livable wage but there is the crappy fitness program."

"I met Kristin and your little grandbaby," I offered. "Kristin said you had a new job. I was surprised to see you here."

"I just had to pack up some personal items. This is all that's left of a long hard story. You can't imagine how happy I am that it's over."

Hmmm, I wondered just how happy she was to have it over. I smiled again and said my goodbyes. There was so much to unpack from that visit. I needed my board and my partners in solving crime to put everything in perspective.

*****

When I got to the house I slipped into the parlor and started writing on the whiteboard. Under Kristin, I added the name "Sam" and wrote *Both Hate the Contis*. Then under Susan I wrote, *Fed up with Contis, moving on.* But something was off. Susan had been teary a couple of days ago when Jimmy's name was mentioned. Today she was angry. Had something changed? Were the feelings just building and we happened to catch her at the end of one grieving stage and the beginning of another?

"Pretty Lady!" a loud voice squawked out of nowhere, scaring the life out of me. I turned around and saw the stupid parrot or whatever it was in a cage in the corner. I had forgotten all about him.

"Who moved you in here?" I wondered out loud.

"Son of a preacher man, son of a preacher man," he answered. I didn't know if that meant Ty or Hitch, and then realized it wasn't really an answer to my question, just a quip the bird brain had memorized. Then again, I would bet my Cuda, Hitch had put him in here like some ornithological version of a wiretap.

"Well I'm sorry you're in here, there's not much light. I'll see about having your quarters updated," I said truthfully but nonsensically.

"Much obliged, pretty lady, pretty lady," he squawked back. I was growing to like this guy.

Under 'Dean Martin' I wrote, *May be angry about Jimmy's lucrative sales business.* At least that is what Shirley said. She was also guessing or deliberately throwing shade. I underlined "May" so I would remember it was just a theory.

Shirley Conti was a bit tougher. She still didn't seem that upset over Jimmy's death, but maybe nine months was enough grieving time. The exhumation didn't seem to faze her at all. I wrote, *Feelings about Jimmy are questionable.*

She also didn't know about the poisoning yet or was Oscar-worthy good at faking it. She might have planted that seed as some sort of plan to cover up what she knew. I added, *starting to suspect (or possibly already knows) death wasn't from natural causes.* Then there was the whole lie about witness protection. Why on earth would she volunteer all that information to a complete stranger? She was either A: planning on running so it didn't matter; B: figured it was all going to come out soon anyway so it didn't matter; C: believed I was on her side for some reason; or D: thought I was so inconsequential that it didn't matter if I knew. Grammar aside, Shirley didn't appear to be stupid, so I guessed it was most likely a combination of A and D. I wrote, *Knew the Olson's; Paid for their burial; Took their identities; and Orchestrated their own escape from Russo.*

Hmmm. I looked at the board, and it felt like everything I had written was a part of a jigsaw puzzle. All the pieces were there, maybe, but I just wasn't quite putting the right shape into the right space. Was it time to take Kendra, Kit, and Beth off? I flipped it back to face the wall and left the parlor, careful to shut the door behind me.

I hustled upstairs to get ready for the picnic and my big swim with Ty. I was convinced Hitch had been the brains behind this proposal. Ty had been a little uneasy when we had kayaked, and I hoped the two of them hadn't bitten off more than we could chew.

I decided a one-piece suit would be more appropriate than a bikini. I chose a navy-blue Ralph Lauren suit with wide white straps and a cute one-shouldered, Yves Saint Laurent red silk sundress. I grabbed the matching strappy red sandals with a big YSL monogram in gold on the top of the foot. Off I went for a day of fun with a bunch of people I hadn't known two months ago, would never have crossed paths with in my former life, and was, oddly enough, looking forward to the whole thing.

*****

Mavis and I were in the front seats of the Explorer. Shawna, her sister Shayla, and Ty were in the middle seat, and Shayna, Ashlee, and Tootsie in her baby bucket were in the third row. We were headed to watch fireworks. Keith, Kelly, and all the little Ks were following us in their van. One of the parishioners had a house on the north end of White Bear Lake and had an annual 4th of July party. He had invited the families at the shelter to join the party and to watch fireworks from his beach. Hitch had the bike and was going to meet us.

I couldn't believe every one of the kids was awake and raring to go after their long day. The picnic had been a big hit, and the pond had been successfully crossed. Hitch swam on one side of Ty and me on the other. Keith followed close behind in the rowboat. I showed Ty how to switch from a front stroke to a backstroke to save energy. You would have thought he had conquered Kilimanjaro, he was so excited.

There was a public parking lot about eight blocks from where we were headed, so we parked there. We waited for Keith and Kelly to get a big double stroller out of their trunk and get all their Ks sorted. Ashlee put Tootsie in a backpack carrier. *Wow, having kids seemed like a lot of work*, I thought.

Just as everyone was finally set, Hitch rolled up. We all took off together. The streets were packed with people all headed towards the lake. They had a big show planned, I was told, and thousands of people came to houses and businesses all around the lake to watch the festivities.

"Hey, Vivi!" I heard from across the street. I looked up and saw Arthur Gottfried waving at me. Arthur was a guy I had dated several times who looked like a surfer but was a few waves short of high tide. Hitch and I crossed to say hello as the rest of the group kept going.

"Hey Arthur," I said.

"Where are you guys headed?" he asked.

"A friend has a house on the north end; we're headed over there," Hitch said.

"Dude, no way, me too. You're so lucky his house is on this side of the lake so you get to see the front."

"The front of what?" I asked.

"The fireworks," Arthur said.

"I don't know what you mean," I admitted.

"I watch them from up here every year. They're always stellar because they shoot them up facing this direction ya know. The people on the south side see the back of them."

Hitch and I just stood there. I assumed his mind was doing the same acrobatics mine was. It started with, *what the hell is he talking about?* Then quickly moved to, *noooo, is he serious?* And I was now struggling with, *what can I possibly say to that?*

"Yep, we're lucky," Hitch said, grabbing my arm and pulling me back across the street.

"Happy 4th," I said over my shoulder.

When we were out of hearing distance I stopped, and grabbed Hitch's arm, "I don't, I mean I can't even, I, uh, there are no words." And we both burst out laughing.

CHAPTER 9

Wednesday

I was in the kitchen pouring myself a cup of coffee when the house phone rang. It made us all jump because we had only heard it a couple of times before.

"Grace in the Valley Shelter," I answered.

It turned out to be Kelly O'Malley, one of the MoGOs inviting me over for coffee which was very sweet. I threw on a cute navy and white Ulla Johnson sundress and a pair of Alexandre Birman white slide sandals.

Kelly lived about seven miles from church in a charming house with sweeping gardens. She was very sweet, and I felt a little guilty that I wasn't really interested in being a part of the MoGOs. She had been a biology professor before she had her two boys and was smart as a whip.

"I made tea. I hope that's alright, I don't drink coffee," she said carrying a beautiful rose patterned tea set out to her patio along with a plate of finger sandwiches and tea cakes.

"Tea is great," I said. "I always assume *going out for coffee* really means a chat and beverage of one's choice," I laughed.

We chatted for a bit and then Kelly said, "So you found the bones, that's interesting. I've known about them for several years, you know."

Kelly dropped this tidbit so casually it was like she was mentioning she had just found a sale on jewelry. I tried to control the look of surprise that undoubtedly had to be on my face.

"You knew about the bones?" I asked.

"Oh, no. I knew about the Olsons not being who they said they were. A few years ago the city was trying to claim eminent domain and take a portion of my parent's land. They live in

Mankato."

"Uh-huh, so how did this lead you to know about the Olsons?" I prodded, as she paused and almost looked like she was rethinking whether or not to finish her story.

"Well, I knew some people had varying degrees of success in St. Paul years ago when they were straightening out Spaghetti Junction. I thought if I could give them a call and ask a few questions maybe they would have a tip for how my parents should proceed. I went to the library and looked at old newspaper articles because I remember having read about a couple who were successful. I found the article and their names were Henry and Sharon Olson. I thought it was interesting that I had recently met a Sharon Olson at church. She was selling designer bags to just about everyone it seemed. I mean it's Olson, so a coincidence sure, but not that odd for Minnesota. I looked up the property records and someone else had the house now. When I bought my Burberry from our Sharon Olson, she said something about her husband Henry. I asked if they had lived in St. Paul and it was the same address.

"When I asked about the city and any tips about keeping them from taking the property she looked like I had asked for directions to the moon. She was inordinately vague and said, 'Oh Henry handled most of that, I'll ask him to give you a call.' Of course, she never called back. I went back to look at the article because there was a picture of them, and it was a couple that was much older and the woman certainly wasn't Sharon. I asked one of the moms in the group if her husband would check into it. He has access to records and info that I couldn't get in the library. He was able to dig up their social security numbers. He said they were the same but the ages were off. He recommended that I forget about it, it was probably a clerical error, so I did. I didn't think about it again until the paper came out this morning. The bones in the belfry were odd anyway and then the paper says it's Henry Olson."

CARRIN MAHMOOD

"Wow, that's crazy," I said. "Whose husband looked into that for you?"

"I'd rather not say," Kelly answered.

"Sure, I get that," I said, remembering Kit saying Kendra's husband was a big wig at the State's Attorney's office and the way Kendra immediately jumped on the phone when Ezzie mentioned the bones.

"Did you say anything to the police?" I asked.

"I didn't see the point, what was I going to say, 'ha-ha I knew two years ago?' They already know all of this info and probably so much more."

"Good point," I conceded.

"This will put a damper on Sharon's traveling I suppose," she added.

"What do you mean?"

"Oh, she travels all over the world. That's how she gets bags at cost. When she's in England she goes to the Burberry factory and buys straight from there. That's how I got this for seven hundred instead of thirteen hundred. It's still kind of extravagant for me but I'm such an Anglophile, I couldn't say no to an actual Burberry."

"So, she goes to Italy and gets the Birkin Bags from the Herme's factory?" I asked.

"Exactly. More tea?" she offered.

Oh man, these women were going to be crushed when they found out they didn't have originals. Kelly's bag was a great knock off but Shirley had probably gotten it for fifty bucks, and most likely her world-travels were only to Seoul where the best quality knock-offs were made. We talked for a bit longer and then I headed back to the house.

It was empty when I walked in so I headed right to the parlor. It was very interesting to me that it was Shirley who was bringing in the big bucks with the counterfeit bags. Was Henry even involved? Did she only sell to the MoGOs and Henry sold to everyone else? She was an odd associate for the MoGOs. I wrote, *Brains of the operation?* under Shirley's picture. Then I wrote *Partner?* I felt like she needed a contact person or some sort of "in" with the group. Who could that be?

The house phone rang for the second time that day and startled me out of my reverie. It was Mangetti.

"Is this Vivi?" he asked.

"Yes, it is," I replied.

"I have some info for ya kid; swing by the Bunker tonight so I can fill you in."

"The Bunker?" I asked.

"Yeah, the joint downstairs, come dressed. The password is 23-skidoo."

"Of course it is," I said.

I looked at the receiver in my hand for a few seconds, slowly realizing that Mangetti had hung up without saying goodbye. I assumed, "come dressed" meant come dressed in period clothes. Good thing I had grabbed the rest of my clothes from the storage unit because I had the perfect dress.

I had attended the *Gangster Gala* last year, an evening supporting local theatres. An up-and-coming local designer, Claire Heizen, had designed my gown. It was a gold beaded drop waist dress with spaghetti straps. It came above the knee and was swingy and fun. I had gold beaded T-strap shoes that matched and a headband with a gold feather.

*****

I wasn't sure I even wanted to go to Mangetti's and was pretty sure I didn't want to go downstairs again. I decided to swing through the parking lot. If there weren't any cars, I would keep on driving. I was counting on lightning not striking in the same place twice as it was, but purposefully and repeatedly walking into the same deserted basement where I had almost died seemed just plain silly.

As it turned out, my fears were unwarranted. The parking lot was packed. There was a door that was painted to look like the stones matching the foundation. I only saw it because I watched a couple walk in ahead of me. "23-skidoo" was indeed the password.

The inside was hopping. The blackjack tables were full as was the roulette table. The one-armed bandits lining the perimeter of the room had waiting lines. There was a jazz combo on the stage with piano, sax, guitar, a drum kit, and a sultry female vocalist. They looked like they stepped right out of the Cotton Club.

My revulsion when I looked at the bar, where I had recently punctured Harold Kramer's testicle with a razor-thin Jimmy Choo stiletto, quickly abated when I didn't see any blood on the floor. Of course it had been cleaned up, it was silly to think otherwise, but near-death experiences made one silly apparently. Besides, the hustling bartenders were busy making their own mess everywhere.

I pulled up the only vacant barstool and looked at the specialty menu. I ordered a gin fizz and asked if Mangetti was around.

BONES IN THE BELFRY

"He'll swing through," the bartender said. "He's still got a full supper club upstairs to deal with."

Holy cow, Mangetti's was a gold mine, I thought. This was a Wednesday; the supper club was full and the speakeasy was packed. I wondered when he found time to help Russo with his extra truckloads of "steaks."

A few minutes later Mangetti did sweep through. He was fun to watch, I admitted. He stopped at every table and greeted people. With a slight head nod or eyebrow raise his staff would bring drinks or appetizers to people. He cheered on a few gamblers as if he was actually hoping they'd win and finally made his way to the bar.

"Miss Luxe," he said, leaning in and kissing me on the cheek, "glad you could make it. Get her a lobster tail with the works and coconut gelato afterward," he told the bartender. I tried to say that wouldn't be necessary but Mangetti just waved my protestations off. I wasn't sure what the protocol was when someone called you and said they had news. Do I pretend I was just there for drinks and lobster or ask for an explanation?

I didn't have to wait long, Mangetti leaned close to my ear and said, "You need to look at the Macutty brothers."

"The slime balls with Mr. Sheffield?" I said, remembering Mangetti's description.

"Yeah. Those two have been throwing money around like it grows on trees lately. Not just in here, but all over town. I mean their business does alright, don't get me wrong, but there's just a way a guy acts when he's spending money he didn't have to work for, ya know what I'm sayin?"

"Sure," I said, thinking about the majority of my former friends and their family money.

"Everyone calls them the *Two-Books Macuttys*, cuz it's no

secret that they do some fancy bookkeeping for their clients. In fact, that's why people choose them. One book for the IRS and one for the vault. I'm not sayin it's your old man's dough they're usin to live like kings, but it sure isn't their money."

"So, do they come in often?" I asked.

"Lawrence and Carole were in this weekend. They had dinner at the club. Then they met Seph and Marlene down here afterwards. Their wives seemed happy, and they were both wearing big ol' brand new guilt-diamonds."

"Guilt diamonds?" I asked.

"Yeah, you know, the kind the old-man buys ya outta nowhere which means he's doin something he shouldn't. And what Seph shouldn't be doin is Delilah."

"Delilah?" I asked. Mangetti just nodded at the band. "You've got to be kidding. That seems rather cliché, that's not really her name?"

"Probably a stage name for this jazz gig, but when Marlene isn't with him, he and Delilah are hot and heavy. I've had to ask them several times to get a room. If you ask me, the old lady knows something's goin on, but the new money that they've been throwin around is too good to care. I'm not saying, I'm just sayin, ya know."

"Got it. Thanks, Mr. Mangetti," I said.

"Hey, you call me Nick. You're like family."

Ergh, did I want to be *like family* with Nick Mangetti? I suppose it was better than the alternative.

"Say, Mr. . . er, Nick, some new friends at church are sporting some pretty fancy designer purses. Birkin bags, Gucci, Tom Ford. They mentioned they got them from Shirley. They seem to think she travels the world for them, but they're knockoffs."

"Kid! Man, I gotta tell ya, you got a good eye on ya. Yeah, old Shirls is making a killin on those, all in that one setting. Now me, I'd be a little nervous cheatin people at church. A little close to the Big Guy, if ya know what I'm sayin. It's a tricky business ya know. You have to market to people who know a Birkin bag from a grocery bag first of all. Then you need an entry point. You can't just walk up to those rich birds with a cart full of purses in the middle of upper-class suburbia like you're the Fuller Brush man, ya see what I'm sayin? Then you have to sell them for enough that it seems like a good deal, but it has to be a believable price. You can't go too low or it screams counterfeit. Then the goods have to be first-rate, good enough to trick discerning shoppers. It's a small target audience but well worth it. Russo gets the best goods out there and, I'm happy to say, he loses a truck full of them now and then if you know what I mean."

I did indeed know what he meant. This was very interesting. First of all, my new Uncle Nick wasn't as unaware of the Contis being in town as he had feigned last week when we showed him the picture of Jimmy the Butcher. He knew all about Shirley selling the counterfeit bags, and he knew they came from Russo. He was also deeply aware of how the counterfeit purse business needed to be run. Were Nick and Shirley in this together or was Shirley cutting into Nick's business? Where did that leave Jimmy? Did Russo know the Conti's were alive and kicking in Minnesota, or did Mangetti work with Russo and just loop them in on his own?

I gave Mangetti my phone number and Ezzie's in case he had more info about any of this. I sat at the bar and ate my lobster with asparagus, au gratin potatoes, and yummy crusty bread. I was too full for gelato and was just about to ask the bartender to put a pint in a bag so I could take it home when the Macutty brothers walked in. I ordered a cup of coffee with Baileys and decided to hang out and take a closer look at the Macuttys.

The floor host welcomed them, and a spot magically opened up at the craps table. I could see they were betting big and losing big. They appeared to not care at all. Mangetti was right, even when you were filthy rich, it hurt a little when you lost your money. Admittedly, I did know more than one high roller who thought worrying about money, let alone worrying in public, was vulgar. But according to Mangetti, they didn't make that kind of money.

When the band took a break the singer slunk over, swinging her hips and her pearls. Seph Macutty cashed out and they moved to a table where she promptly sat on his lap. I didn't think of myself as a prude, but I was uncomfortable watching his hands moving all over her and hers sliding between them. Yuck, I'd seen enough. I remembered to get my gelato to go and slipped past Lawrence near the restrooms as he was pushing his own conquest up against the wall.

I couldn't wait to get back and put all my new info, well new questions, on the board.

CHAPTER 10

Thursday

I chose a simple Akris Punto, sleeveless, white dotted swiss, shirtwaist dress with a wide skirt, and wide leather belt to wear to this week's MoGO gathering. The Gianvito Rossi asymmetrical sling sandals were perfect with their two-and-a-half-inch chunk heel.

The sun was beating down and it was already sweltering when I crossed the parking lot towards church. It was supposed to top out near one hundred degrees. Storms were predicted for the afternoon, and it felt like I was swimming my way across the parking-lot the humidity was so high. As I was cutting between a Navigator and Escalade the buckle on my sling gave out and I kicked my shoe under the Escalade. I was crouched down on one foot trying to reach the stupid sandal when I heard a car door slam and loud voices, clearly continuing an argument that had started in the car.

"... working how you planned," a woman's voice said.

"Hey Kristin, don't walk away from me." I was pretty sure that was Sam, Kristin's boyfriend, doing the yelling.

"Sam, this is going to blow up in our faces. People are looking into this. It's not fair to my mom," Kristin said.

"I'll tell you what's not fair, that son-of-a-bitch lived all these years on Nob Hill while his daughter lives in a fu..."

Beep! Beep! Beep! I interrupted the fight when I inadvertently grabbed the door handle of the Escalade. My foot sizzled every time I tried to put it on the hot asphalt as I was trying to keep my balance on one sandal.

"What the hell?" Sam said coming around the vehicle.

"Oh hi," I said, standing on one foot like a demented flamingo. "I've been trying to get my sandal. It came off and I kicked it under here, but I can't seem to. . ."

Before I could finish my sentence, Sam had dropped onto his belly and reached under the beast for my shoe.

I leaned against the Navigator to put it on and that alarm went off too. Finally, two of the moms poked their heads out of the church and turned off the honking. We all pretended I hadn't interrupted a fight as I awkwardly continued to buckle the stupid strap without touching any metal around me.

"Hey Kristin," I said, breaking the silence, "I noticed all, or er, um, some of the MoGO moms have gorgeous designer bags. I hear someone does a lot of traveling and gets them for a discount. You don't know where I can get one do you?"

"Trust me, you don't want one," she said.

"Oh, shoot, I've always wanted a Birkin bag," I said, trying to sound wistful.

"They're about twenty percent off the original price because Shirley gets them abroad," Kristin said.

"But you would have to work with Shirley," Sam added, "and if I have anything to say about it her bag days will soon be over."

"Oh, my goodness Sam, don't say things like that," Kristin said to him and then turned to me and said, "Ignore him, he's just getting home from the graveyard shift and he's cranky."

Kristin sighed and reached into the back seat of the running car to get the baby out. Sam came over and gave her a big hug. They stood with their foreheads together for a few seconds, he kissed the baby then hopped in the car and left.

That Sam was a multifaceted character, I thought. Kristin and I walked into church together. She went to put the baby in the nursery, while I headed to meet the moms. The treat this week was a box of assorted pastries from *La Boulangerie Marguerite*. I guess homemade wasn't a rule. I selected a jelly-filled pastry of wonder but couldn't stop thinking about Kristin and Sam. I figured Kristin knew about the bags since she had grown up with the Conti's. What was that fight all about? What wasn't 'working how they planned?' Who 'lived on Nob Hill?'

"Take your seats, ladies," Beth said, her voice going a little shrill.

I noticed a huge vase of flowers next to the chair I had been sitting in the week before. I wasn't sure if I should find another place to sit.

"Oh, those are for the shelter," Kelli said. "My garden is going crazy with lily's right now."

"Wow, thank you. What a beautiful variety, that must be some garden," I said.

"Thank you, we do love it," she answered.

*****

Two hours later we were gathering our things and chit-chatting as we were walking out. I hadn't learned anything more than I had the week before. I was walking with my flowers thanking Kelli again, and I thought it's now or never.

"Beth, I have a couple of questions about your purse," I said.

"Oh, Sweetie, it's a Birkin bag. Not to be mean or anything but a girl who lives in a homeless shelter really can't afford one," Beth cooed, patting my arm.

"Works," I said.

"I'm sorry? What did you say?"

"I work at the homeless shelter," I said.

"But you live there, too, right? Honey, I paid thirty thousand dollars for this bag, I'm guessing we don't pay you that much in a year."

Slapping people in the church "narthex" didn't seem right, so I decided to see how deep I could encourage Beth to bury herself instead. "You're saying that bag is worth thirty thousand dollars?" I asked innocently.

"No, it's worth seventy thousand, I just paid thirty. I'm getting another one today."

Well let's see how Miss Beth likes a slice of reality, I thought. "I wouldn't. Even if that one was real, the gold satchel only went for twenty-four thousand and, trust me, that one's not real."

"It absolutely. . ."

"Is a fake." I cut her off, "they all are." I noticed some of the other moms were coming out of the nursery with their kids and had stopped dead in their tracks.

"Well, I'm sure you have no idea. . ."

"Oh, I do have an idea. There are no showrooms at the Hermes factory, or the Burberry factory or any of the others. They have flagship stores, where the bags sell for top dollar, not twenty percent under. These are really good knock offs, but they are knock-offs. These designers just don't discount their stuff. Ever."

"Just shut up Vivianna. You come in here jealous because you don't have a pot to piss in and try to make the rest of us feel bad. You are nothing but a bitch, you are not welcome in this group. . ."

"Whoah, whoa, whoa, what's all the yelling about?" I

heard Hitch saying. He had come out of his office and was taking long strides across the narthex towards us.

"Your house servant is trying to make us feel bad by calling us stupid," Beth said.

"First of all, someone gave me a sock and set me free, so I'm no longer a *house servant*," I said, fully recognizing that she was probably not the type to have read Harry Potter and the reference would be lost on her. "Secondly, I never said you were stupid. I was trying to stop you from buying a second fake Birkin bag for an exorbitant price. I was . . ."

"They're NOT FAKE!" Beth screamed.

"Okay Crazy Pants, take it down a notch," I said to Beth, waiting for her head to start spinning around.

"Ladies, let's settle down," Hitch said.

I just looked at him. "I am perfectly calm."

"Are you serious?" Kendra asked.

"Yes, I am calm as can be."

"No, I mean, are you serious about the bags?"

"I'm so sorry, but I'm afraid so," I said.

The women all looked a little pale except for Kelli. She was not one bit surprised.

"I am sorry Pastor Hitchmayer, but I just won't stand for someone coming into our group and upsetting everyone with her lies."

"Hitch, I'm not lying," I insisted.

"Alright, why do you think these bags aren't real?" Hitch asked.

"Well, see here, the stitches aren't perfectly even, and look, some of the hardware is tarnishing. Hermes only uses precious metals which NEVER tarnish. I could hear the toggle clicking when the bag was being opened," I said, pointing at another bag, "huge giveaway. Birkin toggles are soundless. They are perfectly designed and constructed, and never make noise. Ever." Then I pointed to another bag, "Look how that zipper-pull hangs down, Birkin zipper-pulls stay straight and parallel to the zipper. Always! Hermes has never used that ivory-color lining. And look at this logo. It's too blocky and slightly off-center, the stamp is way too deep and that font hasn't been used since the 90s."

Hitch looked at the different bags as I pointed out each flaw and said, "Well, couldn't any of this be normal deviations from bag to bag?"

"No, actually. Never. That's why Hermes and these other companies are able to charge twenty to two hundred thousand dollars for a purse. They just don't let them out the door with flaws."

"Well, *Little Miss Homeless Shelter*, what do you think about this?" Beth asked, pulling out a faux authenticity card.

"Beth, Hermes would never use a tacky authentication card," I insisted. "They are Hermes. They don't stoop to authenticating. It would be like asking Jackie Kennedy to wear a name tag. You either know her or you don't."

"You're telling me these bags go for how much?" Hitch asked, looking incredulous.

"Well these particular bags are exceptionally nice knock-offs. They probably cost fifty dollars to make, which is a lot in the faux bag game. And I don't think it's our business to ask how much everyone paid," I added hoping to spare some feelings and embarrassment.

"You bitch!" Beth spat.

"Beth, that's unnecessary," Hitch said. "If Miss Luxe is correct, and I'm guessing she is, she's not the one you should be mad at. Who sold these to you?"

"We all bought these from Sharon Olson," Kit Carlson said.

Hitch turned and looked at me, narrowing his eyes with one of his cranky looks. Hmm, someone was good at math. He put two and two together pretty fast. He immediately let it slide off his face and turned to the rest of the group. "Ladies, I'm sure you can get these authenticated somewhere, and if what Miss Luxe says is true, I encourage you to call the police."

"Of course, I knew all that, I've known since I got it. I don't need some little wanna-be authenticating anything for me," Beth said, practically spitting she was still so mad.

"I'm sorry Beth, you were talking about getting another one and I wanted to make sure you knew. Especially if you were going through Shirley again, I didn't want you to be sorry."

"Oh, I'm not the one who's sorry. As I said, I've known all along," Beth said, spinning on her heels and walking into the nursery to get her kids.

I saw Kristin standing at the edge of the room with her eyes huge, still watching all the women. I hoped her mom wasn't involved in all of this.

I headed across the lot back towards the shelter. There were two cars there I didn't recognize, which probably belonged to the Food Squad, and Ezzie's car. Oh oh, that couldn't be good news.

Ezzie was in the kitchen when I walked in. I set the bouquet of lilies on the big marble island, ran over and gave her a huge hug, and said, "I have so much news for you, but first please tell me how it went with Stephen."

"Well, he wasn't thrilled, he wanted details that I refused to give and we decided to leave things as they are and talk again in the fall."

"That's it?"

"Yeah, it's hard to get worked up too much over a relationship where we only see each other every three months. Fyndham is a whole bunch of fun, but who knows where that will go."

"And you've always had Stephen as a backup," I added.

"Yeah, that too."

Mavis came over for lunch and afterward we headed into the parlor to look at the board.

"Wow, you've been busy while I was gone," Ezzie said, looking impressed.

"Yeah, and I hated every minute of it. I needed you two," I said. I told them about the dust-up with Beth after the MoGO session.

"So, do you think she knew from the beginning they were fakes and never said anything to save face?" Ez asked.

"I don't know. Mangetti mentioned that one would need an entry point, maybe she was it. Kristin knew, of course. She looked a little freaked out, although in her defense Beth's tirade freaked everyone out," I said.

"Except Kelli Reese," Mavis added. "I was watching from my desk. She didn't bat an eye when you said the bags were knock-offs."

"Yeah, I noticed that too. What do you think that means?" I asked.

"I'm just saying you didn't deliver any news she wasn't aware of, that's all," Mavis said.

"Two or possibly three of the moms knew before today that the bags weren't authentic," Ezzie said.

"Well, one of them was Kristin, and she never bought one.

She only knew because she lived with the Conti's."

"So who seems more guilty, the mom who threw a fit or the mom who was too calm?" Ezzie asked.

"I don't know if either of them is guilty of anything. But I do know Shirley made at least a hundred grand just from the women in that room. Kelly O'Malley knew there was something fishy going on with the Olsons, and I'm pretty sure Kendra knew more than she was letting on because her husband looked into it. Maybe more of them knew," I said.

"Oh write 'one hundred grand' under Shirley," Ezzie said. I did and all the other things we had figured out under the other MoGOs.

"And Mangetti," I added. I filled them in on our conversation from the night before. "He's either working with Shirley or he's the competition."

"Which means Russo is either working with them both, or just with Mangetti," Mavis said.

"Which means we don't know more about him at all," I added. "Also, Sam and Kristin were fighting on the way into church. Sam seemed hot under the collar." I told them about the partial conversation and the car alarms going off. I wrote, *Not working how we planned*, and *Living on Nob Hill while his daughter lives...*

Then we all stood back and looked at the board.

"You know we started this board to try and figure out who brought bones to the bell tower. Are we trying to figure out who poisoned Jimmy now?" Ezzie asked.

"Well it's probably the same person, don't you think?" Mavis said.

"We're missing something," I said, not really paying attention to what Mavis and Ezzie had been saying.

"I feel like it should be as plain as the nose on my face but I can't put my finger on it," Mavis added.

"That's it!" I said. "Kristin's nose. She's Jimmy the Butcher's daughter. That's why Sam was mad. Jimmy and Shirley were living in the lap of luxury, and his daughter lives in a trailer park on the edge of town"

"So, your dad lets you live in poverty, who's madder about that? You, your baby daddy, or your mom?" Ezzie asks.

"You think Susan poisoned Jimmy?" I asked.

"Well, she had opportunity and motive," Mavis said.

"I feel like we have so much more information than we had a week ago, but it just makes more people look guilty," I said.

"Well let's walk away. We can look at it again after dinner," Mavis said.

I grabbed Ezzie's arm to hold her back and said, "I added some stuff about the Macutty brothers to the back of the board." I filled her in on everything that had happened at the Bunker.

"I think that's a really good start.We will get to the bottom of this, I have no doubt about that," she said. "But Vivster, don't get your hopes up, this might not happen overnight."

*****

We were all huddled in the basement. The hot, humid weather had produced a quiet eerie green sky, which had led to the inevitable tornado sirens. The protocol for the shelter was to hit the basement if the sirens went off. Luckily the basement was huge, and the fourteen of us weren't cramped.

"I have to bring one thing from home that we can add to

an obstacle course," Shayna told us.

"Like what?" Ty asked.

"Like balls you have to bounce, or a hula hoop you have to spin, or a step stool to step up and down. But we don't have that kind of stuff."

She looked pitifully forlorn, so I jumped in. "Well, this is your home, so let's look around the basement while we wait for the all-clear."

"Hey here's a bucket of nails, you could throw them on the ground and have kids try and run through them without stepping on any," Ty said enthusiastically.

"Let's try and find something with less puncture potential," I said.

"How about this ladder, they could lean it against the building, and. . ."

"Ty," I interrupted, "that would be way too dangerous for kids."

"Well is this a camp for pu. . ."

"Language!" Shawna cut him off.

Dang, she was good at that, I thought. "Hey, you could lay the ladder on the ground and have kids step into each of the spaces," I told her.

"Yes!" she said, with her fists in the air, dancing around like Rocky Balboa at the top of the staircase.

"I guess that's the winner," I laughed.

"Ty, help me carry this up," Keith said, grabbing one end of the ladder.

Our phones indicated that the coast was clear so we headed back up the stairs. Ty and Keith brought the ladder outside, and I went to grab some snacks out of the kitchen. I was popping bags of popcorn and found some brownies, homemade granola bars, and apples and put them on the counter.

"You're the best cooker ever," one of the little Ks said.

"Awww, thanks," I laughed. "No one has ever called me that." *With good reason*, I admitted to myself.

Ashlee put Tootsie on the island and she rolled and scooted herself toward the center. Wow, I thought, she is on the move. I had no idea if this was typical or not, but it was kind of fun to watch. Like someone else's puppy.

"Don't let her grab the flowers!" Kelli said. "They're poisonous."

"What?" I yelped. "I brought poisonous flowers into the house?"

"Well yeah, lilies are toxic; but it's fine, we'll just keep them up high."

Well, well, well, I thought. This sheds an interesting light on the unruffled Mrs. Reese. She grows poisonous flowers. How did one even poison someone with a flower? You couldn't just walk up and stuff a tulip in their beak. I suppose you could grind it up or something. I didn't know what kind of poison killed Jimmy but Kelli also said they had huge gardens so if not the lilys I bet they had all sorts of chemicals that would work.

Geez, being mad about getting swindled on a purse was one thing, but would anyone be so mad they murdered for it? It seemed like a leap, but I thought I better put it on the board so I could tell Mavis and Ez.

As I approached the parlor I noticed the door was open and Hitch was standing inside. I had never had my inner voice scream "RUN!" louder than it was yelling at that moment. I tried to tiptoe past the door.

"Vivi," Hitch said without turning around, "Can you come in here for a moment?"

Can I? I thought. I mean sure I was capable, but was I willing? Some crazy person wearing my feet turned and headed into the lion's den. I shut the door behind me. The kids didn't need to witness anything that was about to happen; they had enough crisis in their lives.

Hitch continued to stare at the board with one arm crossed over his chest and his other elbow resting on that arm, his thumb and finger across his mouth, the rest of his fingers curled under his chin looking ponderous. I walked up next to him and said, "I took the families to the basement, just like the shelter manual says."

"You read the shelter manual?" he asked without turning his attention away from the board.

"I wouldn't have mentioned anything if I knew there was going to be follow-up questions," I said.

Shayna had actually been the one who told me, but now wasn't the time to mention that a ten-year-old had read the shelter manual and I still hadn't gotten around to it.

"Does Fyndham know about all of this?" Hitch asked.

I thought of a million evasive and clever answers but decided a straight one might be my best bet. "Probably not. Ezzie was out of town until today and most of the interesting details just went up this afternoon. Also, the last time she tried to tell him something he said he was perfectly capable of running his own investigation, and we should leave it to the professionals."

"Which you seem incapable of doing," he stated. "Vivi. . ."

"Yeah--yeah," I interrupted, "stay away from this, I know, blah, blah, blah." He raised one eyebrow and gave me that soul-piercing look. Hmmm, maybe one too many "blahs."

"Thank you for not yelling at me," I said, sounding a tad pitiful even to my own ears.

"I have never raised my voice to you," he said exasperated.

"Well of course not. If you had raised your voice I'd be out of here. Getting 'yelled at' isn't about literal yelling. It's not a volume situation, it's an attitude situation."

"Then why can't women just say, 'don't be mad at me,' or 'why are you mad?' or 'thank you for not being mad,' instead of saying 'don't yell at me.' You do know what yelling means don't you?"

"Yes, but we sense the spirit in which the message is delivered and, in our head, it's yelling."

"Good grief. How do we stand a chance against that kind of logic?"

"That's your burden, Buster."

CHAPTER 11

Friday

I tossed and turned most of the night. The minute the sun cracked through my blinds I jumped up. I called Ezzie and asked her to hurry over. The breakfast squad was just rolling in when Ezzie pulled up. I had bagels toasted and a dollop of cream cheese on a plate for each of us, along with a huge handful of blackberries. I poured two cups of coffee, handed Ezzie her breakfast, and she followed me into the parlor. I filled her in on the poisonous flower angle.

"I kept vacillating between one person on the board to the next. Beth is a horrible human being who said she knew the bags were fakes. But did she know or was she saving face?" I asked. "And if she did know, was she mad enough to kill someone?"

"And the same with Kelli Reese, only she actually grows poisonous flowers," I continued.

"True, but the reality is she could just be growing flowers and they happen to be poisonous. She may not be growing them for their poison," Ezzie pointed out rationally.

"Good point, but she has easy access to poison and motive," I argued.

"Does she though? Are we sure she knew about the bags?"

"Not positive, I guess. And if poison is as common as a lily, I guess anyone could have easy access."

"Kristin is probably mad that she was never recognized as Jimmy's daughter," Ezzie said.

"Sam seems like the hothead in the relationship," I pointed out.

"And Susan put up with being 'the other woman' for over twenty years, so she could have been fed up," Ezzie added.

"Sure," I agreed, "but Shirley had to put up with 'the other woman' for over twenty years, maybe she had had enough."

"Or maybe Russo found them," Ez said.

"Yeah, I've been thinking about that. What crime boss takes the time to poison someone?" I asked.

"Good point," Ez agreed. "But I only know about crime bosses from TV and movies."

"Fair enough," I said. "What about Mangetti? Don't you find it odd he's always in the middle of our investigations? What are the odds of him being innocent every time?"

"Well, in his defense, this is only the second one. And he's been really forthcoming with information."

"Yeah, but is it good information or information to get us to go down the wrong path?" I asked. "He definitely knew about Shirley selling bags. He didn't seem mad, so I still don't know if he was in cahoots with her or not. Is he the supplier or is Russo?"

"Ugh. I can see why you couldn't sleep."

As we stood and stared at the board we heard a huge crack of thunder and all the lights flickered but stayed on. I could hear the kids traipsing down the steps, and we went to hang out with everyone while they ate breakfast.

"Where are you going today?" I asked Ty.

"We get to tour US Bank stadium and meet some Vikings. And we get to go into the locker rooms, the rich-people suites, and even go on the field."

"Wow, that sounds cool." He had been excited every day. They had toured both Target Field where the Twins played and Target Center where the Timberwolves played on Monday. On Tuesday they went to the new Saints ball field in downtown St. Paul and Wednesday toured Allianz Soccer Stadium. Yesterday had been his favorite. They had gone to the Excel Energy Center. It was ready for a concert, not hockey since it was July, but they got to watch a band load-in and set up their staging.

"I'll help you carry the ladder over to the church," Ty said to Keith. I had noticed that he followed Keith around a lot. I think he missed male attention.

"Sorry man, I'm flying right now, I've got to get to work." He kissed Kelli, the baby-K, and headed out the door.

"We'll help you," Ez said to Ty.

"We will?" I said, a little surprised at her.

"Sure, then we can ask Mavis to borrow the Explorer and snoop around. . ."

"Ah-hem," I interrupted.

"I mean *visit* Kristin and see how she's doing with that cute baby."

*****

Forty five minutes later we were pulling into the trailer park. We parked a few trailers down from Sam and Kristin's. It was still raining so Ezzie crawled over all the seats and dug through a trunk organizer box that Mavis had in the way back of the behemoth she called a car.

"I could only find one umbrella," she said.

"It's okay, we'll share."

I locked the door and gave the keys to Ez because I didn't have pockets. It didn't seem like a mission for a purse. We crouched under the umbrella and headed for Kristin's home.

"I might need to get an 'incognito car' for us to use," Ez

said.

"How many bodies do you think I'm going to find?" I asked her.

"You never know," she said.

We came up to the backside of the trailer. There were no lights on and it was quiet. We walked around to the front and squished together as we went up the few steps to the door. We huddled under the umbrella but no one came to the door. I realized we both had on dark skirts and white tops and probably looked like soggy Jehovah's Witnesses huddled on the tiny porch. *At least it was a good way to assure no one would bother us,* I thought.

"Well that's disappointing," Ezzie said.

We headed down the steps, and I noticed a small storage shed. "Do you think that shed is theirs or the trailer's in the next lot?" I asked.

"It has the same white siding and black trim as theirs," Ezzie said.

We went over to take a look at it. It had a window on one side and double doors in the front with a padlock. I yanked on the lock and the whole latch fell off with the padlock still attached. It had rusted to the point of being worthless, it only gave the impression that it was a locked door.

"Vivi, what did you do?" Ez asked with big eyes.

"I just gave it a tug, not even that hard."

"Well it's open now, we might as well get out of the rain," she said, stepping inside and taking the umbrella with her. She was my best friend, so I had no choice but to follow.

The little shed was packed. There were plastic storage bins along the back, a snowblower, a lawnmower, snow shovels, garden shovels, rakes, and a hose along the wall to the left. *There were literally more yard tools than yard,* I thought. I opened a large box and it was full of Christmas bulbs.

"This feels wrong," I said. "It's just their personal stuff."

"Yeah," Ezzie agreed, opening a box full of baby clothes. "Just check that one and. . ."

I couldn't make out what she was saying because the rain had started falling so hard on the metal roof it drowned out everything else. She was pointing at a huge cardboard box to my right. It was approximately a four-foot cube. I unfolded the flaps and peered inside.

"Unbelievable," I said, pulling out a grey nylon Nike bag.

"Do you think they feel?" Ezzie asked me.

"Feel what?" I said.

"ARE THEY REAL?" she yelled over the rain.

I brought one over to her and we both examined it. "I don't know enough about Nike to say if these are real or not," I admitted.

"The swooshes are right side up," she added, shrugging her shoulders.

I pulled the box away from the wall and a wooden handle fell forward. I handed Ez the bag and grabbed the handle. It was a sledgehammer.

"Do normal people just have these in their garages and sheds?" I asked her.

She shrugged her shoulders again, and then I heard a voice yell, "HEY! What the hell are you doing in my shed?"

Crap! Ezzie started grabbing Christmas bulbs and flinging them as fast as she could at Sam who had driven up unheard because of the rain. He handily batted them away, so she gave up on that line of defense, grabbed the umbrella, and popped it open. She put it in front of her and ran out with one shoulder down like she was pushing her way through the frontline of the Vikings. I should have let her run interference and followed in her swath but I panicked.

"Hey, I know you guys, you're from the church," Sam said, sounding confused. I started twirling in a circle with the sledge-hammer to get momentum, pretty sure I had the exact form of the guys doing the hammer throw in the Olympics. I spun out of the door and aimed it at Sam, but was belated in letting go. He took a small step sideways with a baffled look on his face while the weight and momentum of the sledgehammer yanked me off my feet pulling me across the now muddy yard. I slithered in the mud on my belly like I was on a slip-and-slide. Mud was flying in my face and making a rooster tail behind me.

"Eeek," I squeaked.

"What the hell?" Sam said.

"Vivi, run!" Ezzie yelled, all at the same time.

I scrambled to my feet and took several frantic steps in place feeling like a cartoon going nowhere. Finally, I slipped and slid until I got to the road. Ezzie left the now inside-out umbrella behind as she clicked the fob for the Explorer to unlock. We dove into our respective doors and she got the key in the ignition and tore out of the trailer park.

"Crap!" she said.

"Yup," I agreed.

"So that is the same bag you found in the belfry, right?" Ez said.

"Yup," I agreed again.

"And I bet the sledgehammer broke into the mausoleum,"

she added.

"Uh-huh," was all I could manage.

We headed back towards the shelter not saying anything. When we pulled into the lot I suddenly remembered the conversation I had with Sam and Kristin the morning before. I said, "We need to warn Shirley."

"Why Shirley?" Ezzie asked.

"Yesterday when I ran into Sam and Kristin, interrupting their argument, I asked where I could get a Birkin bag. Sam made some threatening remarks against Shirley."

"Sure, but let's get dry clothes on first."

I took the fastest shower of my life to get the mud off. The rain had cooled things down so I opted for a pair of black Kate Spade cargo pants and a Ralph Lauren white summer sweater. Ezzie borrowed a pair of knit straight-legged pants which she cuffed once to turn into capris and a kelly green silk knit summer sweater. *Days like these that started in the nineties and dropped to the sixties were exactly why it was imperative to retrieve the rest of my clothes from the storage unit*, I thought. I'd have to explain this to Hitch.

Ezzie and I jumped into my car because it was clean and dry. I had sent Mavis a text explaining the state of her vehicle with a promise to have it detailed when we came back. She text back saying she would walk over and just wipe the seats off with a towel and not worry about it. Hmm, maybe an 'incognito car' would be handy.

When we pulled up to the Conti's there was a huge, gold '72 Ford LTD in the driveway. I kind of had a thing for vintage muscle cars, and even though this wasn't in that category, the big old boat was cool.

We parked on the street in case the owner of the LTD

needed to get out of the driveway. Ez rang the doorbell several times, and we were just about to go around back and knock when Shirley came to the door.

"Oh, you again," she said when she saw me.

"Hi Mrs. Conti, may we come in? We have some news about Jimmy's death, and you might want to sit down," I said.

"Sure," she said, waving us through, looking curious.

"Mrs. Conti, we know about the counterfeit bags you've been selling. . ."

"Hey, them bags is as real as they come," she said, cutting me off. "I travel around the world, shopping in factory show-rooms to purchase them for twenty percent off. Sure, I add in a little something for the travel, but not much."

"Bullshit," Ezzie said simply.

I gave her a withering look. "Yes, well, we know that's not true," I said. "Everyone knows the bags aren't authentic, so you won't be selling to the moms at Grace in the Valley anymore, but that's actually not the main point of our visit."

"Ya don't say." Shirley said, leaning back in her chair and crossing her legs, "well please, enlighten me. Why ya here then?"

"We've come to warn you that the person who killed your husband is also planning, well probably planning, to harm you also."

"Fascinating, you girls want a cup a joe and some pastry? I just got some napoleons."

"Uh, sure?" I said looking at Ezzie. This was not the re-action I thought we'd get. Then again, she had been married to someone whose nickname ended with "the Butcher" so maybe she just wasn't flappable.

She left us sitting in the living room while she went off to get refreshments. "This is weird," Ezzie said, once she was out of earshot.

I nodded my agreement. The coffee must have been made because she was back with a tray in under five minutes.

"That's beautiful china," I complimented.

"It was a weddin gift," she said.

She poured all three of us a cup, and we fixed ours how we liked it with the sugar and cream she had brought out. "The napoleons are delicious," I said truthfully.

"I'm glad you like 'em. My brother Sal brought 'em in fresh from Chicago this morning. There's a bakery there I use ta go to back in the day, and he knew I loved 'em," Shirley said. As if saying his name conjured him out of thin air, Sal appeared in the doorway.

"Shirls, ya gonna introduce me to your pretty friends?" he said.

"Sure, what's your names again?" she asked.

"Hi, I'm Vivianna, and this is my friend Esmeralda," I said.

"You don't look like an Esmeralda," Sal said.

"I get that a lot," Ezzie said, smiling back.

"So, the girls are sayin my bags aren't the real deal," Shirley said to her brother. I wondered for just a moment if she had been swindled as well and then remembered she told everyone about the showrooms which just wasn't true.

"Ya don't say," Sal said, equally unflapped.

"They say they know who killed Jimmy," she added.

"Now that's mighty interestin," Sal said, coming into the room and sitting on a chair next to Shirley's.

He was a handsome older man, sadly he had gotten the

lion's share of the looks in the family. He was kind of a silver fox and reminded me of the Dos Equis' *Most Interesting Man in the World*, guy.

"I see your suitcases are gone," Ezzie said. "Did you decide to stick around for a while?"

That was out of left field I thought, but Ezzie usually has a method behind her madness.

"Just the opposite actually," Shirley said, "That's why Sal is here. He's helpin me move. I think Russo got wind a me sellin purses and that's his gig ya know. I was doin pretty good so I'm pretty sure he's the one who killed Jimmy. I thought I better skedaddle."

"Well he might not be the one," I said, thinking, *she dropped the "them bags is as real as they get" schtick fast.*

"Ya don't say," she said, sounding a lot like her brother.

"That's why we're here," Ezzie said.

My phone chirped and I saw it was a text from Mangetti. I was going to ignore it, but it was so out of the blue I decided I better read it.

Mangetti: *Russo is in town,*

Vivi: *We're at Conti's, should I warn Shirley?*

"You see, we found stolen Nike bags and a sledgehammer in Kristin and Sam's storage shed," Ezzie was saying.

"Who the hell are Kristin and Sam?" Sal asked.

"That's Jimmy's daughter and her boyfriend."

"You knew she was Jimmy's daughter?" I asked, surprised.

"Well sure, ya seen the schnoz on that girl?" Shirley said.

Huh, this was interesting, I thought. I looked at Shirley and said, "Sam made some threatening remarks against you."

"We are pretty sure he brought the original Mr. Olson's bones up to the belfry and probably killed Jimmy," Ez added.

Mangetti: Sure, but get the hell out of there, I think Russo's on his way, I'll send a pic.

"Um Shirley, you and Sal should leave now. Ez let's go," I said standing up. "Russo is in town."

"Is that so she said," without moving or batting an eye. "Ya hear that Sal, Russo is in town."

"How do you know that kid?" he asked.

"Mr. Mangetti just texted me, he's going to send a picture, and . . ."

The next text interrupted me. I opened it to see what Russo looked like. It was a picture of Shirley's brother. I was confused for a second. It slowly registered that the man sitting in front of us was Russo, and he and Shirley were, at the very least, in the counterfeit-bag selling business together.

Vivi: he's here.

. . . "and what?" Sal asked.

"And we better go, that was the shelter, they need us back right away," I said hoping I sounded calm and that he couldn't hear my heart beating out of my chest.

"Sorry ladies," Sal said, pulling a gun from the waistband in the back of his pants. "Hand me your phone."

I thought about throwing it because I had heard once that you should do that so they had to choose whether they went after the thing they wanted or you. But in that moment I realized how stupid that advice was. What would stop him from shooting me and then walking over and picking up my phone? Not antagonizing him was the best bet, I reasoned.

"I feel real bad about this," Shirley said. "You've been so nice tryin to keep me safe and all. Wasn't that nice Nick?"

"It was real heart warmin," he said. "Now let's go out to the car."

He motioned with his gun that we should start walking. When we got to the driveway, he unlocked the trunk and handed the gun to Shirley and began taking Shirley's suitcases out of the trunk. When he was finished he motioned for Ezzie and me to get in. I got in first and laid on my side facing the opening, then Ezzie climbed in after me and we spooned as he slammed the lid.

We could hear Shirley arguing about bringing all her stuff. She must have won because the next thing we heard was the back door open and the car bouncing as the heavy bags got thrown in. We didn't say a thing until the car was started and a Twins game was blaring from the radio. *They must be playing the White Sox*, I thought inconsequentially.

"Thank God he doesn't drive a Toyota," Ezzie said.

After we got rolling I asked where her phone was.

"It's in my back pocket," she said. Since my hands were closer to her back pocket I started feeling for it. I was able to find it and pull it out.

"Can you kick the tail light out?" I asked.

"I'm working on it."

I called Hitch and he picked up on the second ring. "Hi, Russo and Shirley Conti have us in the trunk of their car," I said.

"What?" he said loudly.

"Look Hitch, I don't have time to repeat everything. We went to Shirley Conti's house and Russo was there, he pulled a gun and made us get into the trunk. Oh, hang on, Mangetti is calling."

"WHAT! Are you freaking kidding me?" I heard him saying as I switched over.

"Hey Mr. Mangetti, It's me, Vivi. I have Ezzie's phone because Russo took mine. We're actually locked in Russo's trunk right now and can't really talk because I have the police on the other line."

"I figured something was wrong when you didn't answer your phone. Don't you worry about a thing," Mangetti said, "Just get back to the police."

I hung up with Mangetti and reconnected with Hitch.

"So how was Mangetti? Did you two have a nice conversation?" Hitch asked.

"He didn't say much," I said. "It was weird, he. . ."

"Vivianna, I don't care what Mangetti said. What the hell is wrong with you?"

"Oh, sorry. Hitch, I'm kind of scared," I admitted my voice cracking.

"Okay, stay with me, don't hang up. I'm giving the phone to Fyndham."

"You're with Jake?" I asked.

"He's with Jake? Ezzie repeated.

"Yeah, I invited him over to look at this board," he said.

"Oh, well we found stolen Nike bags in Jimmy the Butcher's daughter's storage shed. And a sledgehammer. So, we thought her boyfriend probably put the bones in the belfry and killed Jimmy. We went to warn Shirley, but Russo was there. I still think Sam is responsible for the bones, but Russo made us get in his trunk.

"Vivi? Where are you exactly?" Jake asked.

I guess Hitch had handed the phone over at some point during my long story. "I don't know. I mean, we are in the trunk but now we're moving," I answered.

"Where was the car when you were abducted?"

Yikes, *abducted*, I didn't like the sounds of that. Hearing it somehow made this whole thing worse.

"We were at Conti's in Stillwater, we've been driving for a few minutes. Oh, we're turning and accelerating, I think we have to be going onto a freeway," I said.

"Vivi, this is really good, you're doing great. You're probably on I94. I've already called this in. Dispatch is going to be waiting for you, and we will try to ping Ezzie's phone. Highway patrol is informed in Minnesota and Wisconsin, as well as the local guys. We've also got Airwing on this. Can you tell me what kind of car you're in? It's okay if you don't know much, any little details will help."

"It's a gold '72 LTD convertible. Whitetop. 429 V8. White-wall tires, gold hubcaps."

"Wow, good job Viv," Fyndham said. "That's really helpful. We'll find you soon."

"Okay," I said quietly, sounding a bit pitiful.

"You need to try and kick out the taillights. First pull all the wires you can see, just start yanking. You need to get a hand out or piece of clothing so people can see, and then hopefully they'll call it in and it will help us find you."

"Ezzie's on it," I said simply.

"Alright Vivi, can you give Ezzie the phone? I want to talk to her, and then you are going to hang up and call 911 do you understand? You've got this, it's going to be fine."

I held the phone to Ezzie's ear and gave her and Fyndham

BONES IN THE BELFRY

as much privacy as possible considering my chest and stomach were literally up against Ezzie's back. She said goodbye and I could hear Hitch calling my name.

"Vivi, dial 911 and just do whatever they say. This will be over soon."

I hung up and called 911. I repeated what I had said to Fyndham and was transferred to someone who was waiting for the call. They basically repeated the same instructions Jake had just given me.

Ezzie had kicked out the light, and we were trying to figure out how to synchronize our movements so we could get a hand to the brake light opening where her foot had so recently been.

"This trunk is insane," I said, scooting up as much as I could onto a ledge-like platform towards the back of the trunk. "We could invite guests over."

We maneuvered and scooted and I ended up with my head on the opposite end of the trunk and was able to stick my hand out the brake light hole. It was a long narrow opening so my arm fit through up to the elbow. Ez found my other hand and I gave her the phone. She introduced herself to the person on the other end and repeated everything we were doing and hearing.

"He wants to know if you can see anything," Ez said.

I squirmed until I could get an eye up to the opening. "All I can see is the road; no one is close enough to see. I'm sorry I can't see another car, and I can't see into the other lane."

"It's okay, Vivi, you're doing a good job," Ezzie said.

I was assuming we were headed east on 94. They were heading back towards Chicago. How long before it was rural enough that Sal would pull off and get rid of us? I had driven to Chicago several times and farm country started right outside of Hudson. Hmmm, the longer we drove the happier I was he hadn't pulled over. It gave Ezzie and me more time to be rescued.

"Someone saw us. They just got a call; someone saw a gold LTD with someone in the trunk waving out the back," Ezzie said.

I gave a thumbs up to the car that could see my hand and then the ALS sign for love, or possibly 'rock-n-roll' I could never remember which was which. Either way I hoped they got the message.

A few minutes later we heard sirens and could feel the car accelerating.

"He's not going to run from the police, is he?" Ez asked.

"Ugh, I hope not, I can't imagine a car chase will end well."

We heard more sirens, and then thankfully the car started slowing down.

"I hope their idols weren't Bonnie and Clyde," Ezzie said.

I pulled my hand back into the trunk just in case. I didn't want it full of holes. We could hear muffled voices and noises and a thud against the car as it rocked a bit. A few minutes later the trunk opened, and an officer was standing there looking at us.

"Miss Luxe and Miss Gold?" he said.

"Yes," we said at the same time. What if we had said no? I started giggling imagining the look on his face, thinking more than two girls were traveling around in the trunks of big old Fords. I may have been belatedly moving towards hysteria.

Two officers helped us out of the trunk and into the back of a squad. Shirley and Russo were already gone, presumably in the back of a different squad. There were at least a dozen vehicles, marked and unmarked. Traffic had been stopped but was now slowly being funneled into one lane. We started rolling and got to turn around in one of those highway separator paths that only law enforcement gets to use, so that was fun.

More than an hour later we were still in a small room in the Washington County building huddled next to each other. Ezzie and I were holding hands and sitting as close as we could while remaining in our own chairs. No one had said much to us, and we hadn't even said much to one another. I wasn't sure how Ezzie felt, but I was kind of holding on by a thread and just wanted to get home and sit in my shower and cry. Hitch and Fyndham walked in. *Yikes*, I thought, *there were two faces you didn't want to be on the wrong side of.* Of course, that could very possibly be exactly where we were, the jury was still out regarding our good standing.

Ezzie and I stood up, she ran towards Fyndham, who opened his arms, and she burst into tears. I could feel my lip quivering and my eyes filling too. Shoot, I was still miles from my shower and didn't want to lose it here. And I didn't have an "Office-Handcuffs" to melt into.

I turned away from them and looked at Hitch, who took a deep breath, looked at the floor, and predictably started shaking his head. He took a few steps towards me, and I, too, dissolved into a weepy mess, so he pulled me in for a hug that felt way too warm, solid, and wonderful. Crap, my life really was a mess.

We declined the offer of going to the hospital to get checked out. There was nothing physically wrong with either of us. Four hours later we had given a statement regarding the day's events, told them what we knew about counterfeit Birkin bags, of which I was an expert, and Nike bags, which I knew nothing about except the location of where I had seen a huge box full.

We told them everything Shirley and Russo had said, everything Susan, Kristin, and Sam had said, and anything else I had heard in the last two weeks. I left out the part where Mangetti had said he helped Russo out with "extra steaks" now and then. It didn't seem pertinent, and the man had tried to warn us about Russo.

Hitch had waited and was giving us a ride home. The rain had finally stopped and it was a clear evening. Kids were riding their bikes and people were out for a walk. It struck me how insignificant my shenanigans were to the world's everyday existence.

CHAPTER 12

Saturday

Ezzie had stayed overnight, neither of us wanting to be alone. Hitch hadn't said much. I had dropped into bed exhausted and thought I might sleep until dinner, or even into the next day, but it was only eight o'clock and I was wide awake.

I tiptoed downstairs. The breakfast squad was there making French toast, bacon, and cutting up fruit. They had a pot of coffee finished so I helped myself to a cup and went outside on the back porch and curled into one of the big cushioned rockers. A few minutes later I heard the rumble of Hitch's bike, and shortly after that I saw him walking across the lawn.

"You alright?" he asked.

"Yeah," I answered.

"If you give me your keys, I'll go over to Conti's and get your car. Fyndham called, it's not part of the crime scene."

"Thanks." I was thrilled that I didn't have to go there. I never wanted to see that place again.

"Sam admitted that he stole the Nike's from the Conti's. I guess their whole second floor was set up as a showroom for the different bags. Susan knew about the real Olsons and, at some point, had told Kristin, who, of course, had shared it with Sam. He said he and Kristin were sure Jimmy didn't die of natural causes, but Shirley had buried him fast and didn't think anyone would believe them, so thought if the bones showed up someone would eventually look into it."

"Well it worked," I said.

"It sure did," Hitch agreed. "Shirley said it must have been Russo who poisoned Jimmy. Russo is saying it was Shirley. He also tried saying he had no idea the Conti's were even here until a few days ago."

"Sure. You could see that coming a mile away."

"Shirley also confessed that Russo had been using Jimmy for the last twenty years. Jimmy ran his business for him out of St. Paul and Kansas City."

"So why the big subterfuge?"

"I guess Russo liked how Jimmy did business but still wanted to make an example out of him, so gave him a choice, play dead or be dead. He and Shirley have had an affair for almost twenty years."

"Well that explains why she wasn't broken up about Jimmy and Susan I guess. What's her part in this?"

"They're still sorting that out," Hitch said. "Shirley wants to cut a deal and be in real witness protection this time."

"Wow, you sure know a lot about this," I said, squinting to try and figure out what was going on.

"Fyndham called me this morning. I've got to tell you, seeing that Washington County number pop up on my phone makes my heart skip a beat," Hitch admitted.

"Yeah, you and Jake, huh, strange bedfellows."

"Well, he's connected to Ezzie, and apparently when I hired you, Ezzie came along as part of the package, so we might as well get along."

"That's nice," we heard Ezzie say from behind us. She had a cup of coffee for herself and handed one to Hitch. "Here you go Monsignor," she said as she scooted him over and sat next to him on the porch swing. "You will never regret hiring us."

"Mmm hmm," Hitch answered, taking a long sip of his coffee. But his eyes were crinkling a little in the corners.

Ezzie and I grabbed breakfast and moved out onto the lounge chairs. I filled her in on what Hitch had told me, and we chatted about the day before.

"Were you scared?" Ezzie asked me.

"Not as scared as I should have been," I admitted. "More so now."

"Yeah, Russo and Shirley were so polite it seemed a little surreal, more of an inconvenience than something life threatening."

"Until it was," I said.

"Yeah, until it was," she agreed.

*****

Right before dinner, I saw a U-Haul pull into the driveway and a car I didn't recognize pull in behind. I wondered if we were getting a new family. It would be odd that Mavis hadn't warned me, and really strange that they brought so much stuff. I walked out the front door and Hitch hopped out of the driver's side. Ty and another guy I didn't know hopped out the passenger door. Three more men got out of the other vehicle.

"What's going on?" I asked Hitch.

"Come and see," he said. He pulled out the ramp of the truck and undid the latch. When he rolled the door up I saw all my beloved bedroom furniture. My chaise, my desk, all of it. And wrapped in moving blankets was the Neiman.

I burst into tears and Ty said, "Do you like it Vivi or are you mad? Because I told Pastor Hitch we maybe shouldn't go through your stuff."

"Ty, I love it," I said, pulling him in for a hug.

"Okay guys, let's move the stuff from upstairs out first," Hitch said. "I have a feeling we are in for an evening of 'yes ma'am, no ma`am' and a lot of rearranging."

The End

Watch for *Gold in the Garden*, coming out Fall of 2021.

Turn the page for a sneak peek.

GOLD IN THE GARDEN

It had been an eventful summer. I had been minding my own business, living a fabulously luxurious life like a normal person when my dad sneaked out of town in the middle of the night like Simba leaving the Pride Land. From there, things had gotten interesting. I had slept in a storage unit, been hired by a nosey and absurdly handsome pastor to work at a homeless shelter, and found not one but three dead bodies on the church grounds. Well to be fair, one was dead and lying in repose in the mansion-cum-shelter's parlor when I arrived. Yeah I know, believe me, I think it's weird too. The other one appeared by the casket. And the third one was really just a bag of bones which I literally stumbled upon in the belfry. Also, my life had been threatened twice, once by the son of the couple who had donated the shelter to the church, and once by a mob boss and woman selling counterfeit purses. It sounds a little nutty when I lay it all out. Needless to say, I was looking forward to the last week of summer before school started and was hoping that a new season would bring a new, and well-deserved, zen into my life. And it would have, except while I was helping the kids at the shelter bury a time capsule. I found gold in the garden.

ABOUT THE AUTHOR

Carrin Mahmood

Carrin grew up on the east side of St. Paul, in Minnesota in a house where there was always an open book to be found on most flat surfaces. She taught English and Physical Education in Michigan (near the thumb for those of you who know and love Michigan) until the lakes of Minnesota called her home. She has a Master's Degree in Theology, which makes perfect sense for someone who wants to write romance novels and mysteries.

When she's not writing she's cooking a free community meal and running a homeless shelter for families. She and her daughter have a women's adventure group called Women in the Wild. She has one husband, (because that seems about the proper amount) four kids, two grandchildren she adores, and one dopey dog.

VIVIANNA LUXE
MYSTERIES

Vivianna Luxe was born into a magical life of wealth, fast cars, and endless parties. That all came crashing down when her father slipped out of town in the middle of the night because someone was framing him. All assets had been frozen and Vivi found herself hiding out in her storage unit until a distractingly charming pastor had found out where she was staying and offered her a job as a house mother at a family shelter that his church ran.

Vivi wanted nothing more than to find out who was framing her father but kept stumbling upon dead bodies. Her best friend Ezzie is willing to jump into any fray with her, and somehow Mavis the church secretary has become a willing and useful sidekick.

Between the shelter guests, "helpful" church members, a disapproving but yummy lead pastor, and the odd characters that seem to be drawn to Vivi and Ezzie she has to navigate the many foreign quirks of being part of the church, as well as work to figure out an alarming amount of mysteries tied to Grace in the Valley Lutheran Church.

Corpse In The Parlor

Vivianna Luxe was living a perfectly happy life going to galas, fundraisers and soirees. Then in the middle of a spa day her world came crashing down when she found out her dad slipped out of her life in the middle of the night and all their money was gone. She packed up as much of her life as she could into two moving trucks and hid out on the other side of the tracks. When a nosy, and disconcertingly handsome, pastor overheard her tell her best friend she was sleeping in her storage unit, he offered Vivi a job as House Mother at the homeless shelter operated by his church. The perks included a free room at the mansion that was being used as a family shelter and free food. It couldn't have been more perfect until dead guys started piling up. All Vivi wants is to figure out who is framing her dad so she can get back to being filthy rich like a normal person, but first she has to figure out who is responsible for the corpse in the parlor while dodging odd parishioners and keeping her heart far away from her boss.

Bones In The Belfry

Allowing the Grace in the Valley bell tower to be used during a scavenger hunt seemed like a great idea, right up until the House Mother, and one of the kids, from the family shelter, found a bag of bones.

Vivianna Luxe had been hired to be the House Mother for the shelter by a nosey, and disconcertingly handsome, pastor when he learned she was hiding out in her storage unit. The position was temporary because Vivi's real job was figuring out who was framing her father so she could get back to being filthy rich like a normal person. Unfortunately, she kept getting sidetracked by finding dead guys on the church property.

Pooh-poohing any danger, Vivi, her best friend Ezzie, and their sidekick Mavis decide they need to find out how the bones made their way to the belfry. Can they do it despite Mavis being the church secretary, Ezzie's canoodling with the local LEO, and Vivi trying to ignore the decidedly tempting Pastor Hitchmayer and his bothersome overreaction to their meddling?

BOOKS BY THIS AUTHOR

Corpse In The Parlor

Vivianna Luxe was living a perfectly happy life going to galas, fundraisers and soirees. Then in the middle of a spa day her world came crashing down when she found out her dad slipped out of her life in the middle of the night and all their money was gone. She packed up as much of her life as she could into two moving trucks and hid out on the other side of the tracks. When a nosy, and disconcertingly handsome, pastor overheard her tell her best friend she was sleeping in her storage unit, he offered Vivi a job as House Mother at the homeless shelter operated by his church. The perks included a free room at the mansion that was being used as a family shelter and free food. It couldn't have been more perfect until dead guys started piling up. All Vivi wants is to figure out who is framing her dad so she can get back to being filthy rich like a normal person, but first she has to figure out who is responsible for the corpse in the parlor while dodging odd parishioners and keeping her heart far away from her boss.

Soul Mate Undercover

Nikolena Monroe is happily, and competently doing her part to keep a local newspaper solvent when her boss arranges for her to travel to Italy, undercover, to be part of the wildly popular reality show 'Soul Mate.' The problem is that both her column "Nik of Time" and her blog entries have repeatedly ranted about that very show. Now she will be heading to Italy to spy on the snotty contestants, survey the crew, and dish on the star. And she will be doing it with possibly too few shoes, probably too little makeup, and definitely too many secrets. Staying aloof, and professional, is her only chance of getting through this without any attachments. But can she do it, and, in the end, is that what she really wants? Travel with Nikolena as she joins the cast of "Soul Mate" in a stunning backdrop and experience her adventure through narrative, as well as Nikolena's blog entries, newspaper articles and tweets. With snappy dialogue and rich detail you will fall in love with Nilolena and laugh as she tries to avoid falling in love while undercover.

Printed in Great Britain
by Amazon

19392866R00108